Relationship Stories
by
Marty Nemko

Copyright © Marty Nemko, all rights reserved, 2023

Praise for Marty Nemko

"Magnificent food for thought." Walter Block, Wirth Eminent Scholar, Loyola U.

"Delectable bite-sized, short stories…It's difficult to stop reading them." Dr. Mark Goulston, author of *Just Listen*.

"Some unusual subjects to say the least! I highly recommend this worthwhile read." Michael Edelstein, author of *Three-Minute Therapy*.

"One of the few truly original thinkers of our time." Kathryn Riggs, retired, U.C. Berkeley School of Education."

"A really smart person." Michael Scriven, former president, American Evaluation Association.

"The best of the best." Warren Farrell, author, *The Myth of Male Power*.

Marty Nemko

Photo credit: the author

- ✓ Author of 27 books, ranging from *Careers for Dummies* to *Dark: short-short stories of what we whisper about*

- ✓ Ph.D., educational psychology, University of California Berkeley.

- ✓ Loves playing concerts of popular music on the piano, acting in plays, hybridizing roses, and hanging out with his wife, Dr. Barbara Nemko and their sweet doggie, Hachi.

- ✓ Marty's first job was, at age 13, barroom piano player. At 20, he drove a taxicab in New York City.

Contents

Marty Nemko iii
Contents v
Romance: Meeting 1
   Do You Take This…? 1
   Hermiting Together 3
   Knitting 5
   Venus and Iris 7
   Ikebana Circle 11
   Marry? 13
   Cheap Date 15
   My Donut Hole 17
   Secretly Rich 18
   Telemarketer with a Heart 19
   The Collector 22
   Postcards 25
   Opposites Attracting 28
   Hypochondriac 31
   The Prom 33
   Autumn Love 34
   In Tune 35
   A First Date 37
   Looking 39
   My ChatGPT Harem 41
   My Imaginary Wife 43
   I Invited a Dwarf to Coffee 44
   Mabel 46
Romance: Challenges 47
   Which Guy? 47
   Married, Filing Separately 48
   "I *Am* Going to Have the Baby" 50
   Cop in Bed 52
   Pillow Talk 53
   A Sighing Marriage 55

    It All Came Down to the Sex 59
    Kissy-Poo 60
    A Pier 61

Romance: Endings 64
    Seven Kisses 64
    Not Your Usual 50th Anniversary 66
    A Few Hundred Years in Purgatory with My Wife—No
       Biggie 68
    A Couple in Retirement 71
    Birth and Death 75
    "I Wanted My Husband to Die" 77

At Work 79
    A Loyal Gardener 79
    "The Bitch" 81
    "It's Not My Job to Make You Coffee" 82
    Fired 84

Family 86
    Spoon 86
    Story Time 89
    Empty 91
    Lip Gloss 92
    Wonder Woman 94
    Playing Hooky 95
    Who to Save? 97
    Mother of the Bride 99
    My Daughter is Getting Married 100
    An MD and His Starving-Artist Child 102
    A Gen Z Son Fights His Millennial Dad 104
    Father's Day 106
    Hide 107
    An Empty Nester 109
    Like Mother, Like Daughter? 111
    A Pregnant Nod 113
    A Terrible Two 115
    Bully 117
    Mush 120

Buried Treasure	121
Friends	**122**
The Broken Hearts Club	122
My Hero	124
Following Church Teachings	126
The Garden Club	128
The Hillcrest Widow Club	130
Dogs	**132**
Kisser	132
Second Love	135

Romance: Meeting

Do You Take This…?

Paula and Justin met on Coffee Meets Bagel, attracted to each other by shared interests, both having middle-income jobs, both liking to think things through, and most of all, finding each other attractive but not so attractive that they'd often be hit on.

Marko Milivojevic, Pixnio, Free to use

After the requisite first check-out over coffee, there was the movie date, the dinner date, then the dinner-plus-dessert date. A few months later, they moved in together and soon decided to marry. There was no drama, such as one person wanting to tie the knot, the other unsure. They were at the age when the peer and parental pressure plus a desire to finally be grown-ups and to have kids, all sprinkled with pixie dust, made Paula and Justin's decision easy.

Although neither Paula nor Justin were religious, they knew that at least some invitees would prefer a church wedding while even the atheists would just shrug. So First Lutheran it was. After all, Pastor Christine had baptized Paula.

So there were Paula and Justin at the moment of truth: the vows. The pastor didn't rush through them. She allowed plenty time for the couple to let each of those time-honored phrases fully soak in.

And indeed, both Paula and Justin, consistent with their liking to think things through, reflected on each phrase as the minister said them:

(Paula's thoughts are in *italics*.)

"Do you Paula Whitney take Justin Novak to have and to hold from this day forward…"

"The sex is still good, although not as good..."

"For better, for worse…"

"Kathy and Tom seemed so perfect and now they're divorcing."

"For richer, for poorer,"

"What if Justin quits to work for a nonprofit?"

"In sickness and in health…"

"Mary left Charlie when his MS got bad. What would I do?"

"To love and to cherish, till death do you part?"

"Forever is an awfully long time."

After just a wisp of hesitation, to unconsciously compensate for her doubts, she exclaimed, "I do!"

(Justin's thoughts are in *italics*.)

"And do you, Justin Novak take Paula Whitney to have and to hold, from this day forward…"

I have a roving eye. I haven't cheated yet but…

"For better, for worse…"

"Peter and Trish are exhausted by their kids."

"For richer, for poorer..."

"*Trish told Peter she always wanted to work but then...*"

"In sickness and in health, "

"*What if Paula got cancer? What if I did?*"

"To love and to cherish, till death do us part."

"*Forever is an awfully long time.*"

Having heard Paula's hesitation, Justin too jumped right in with an assertive, "I do!"

"I pronounce you husband and wife."

Everyone applauded.

Hermiting Together

Raw Pixel, CC1.0

I don't much like people and they don't much like me.

In romance, I find them more trouble than they're worth. You have to compromise on what to do, what temperature to keep the room, how and how often to have sex.

More generally, I find most conversations boring — travel, family, pop culture. And when people talk politics, most are too cocksure. They'll listen — usually politely, occasionally not— to what I have to say but rarely if ever change their mind. Neither do I — I usually dismiss their thinking as illogical or at best, short-sighted.

So I found myself becoming more and more hermited. And the less the people contact, the happier I found myself. I fill my time more pleasurably with work, binge-watching, and my hobbies: magic tricks, herb gardening, and most of all, reading. I get higher-quality people contact by reading authors' considered thoughts on all manner of things. I usually read a few books at a time and just pick up whatever I'm in the mood for. Currently, I'm reading Walter Isaacson's *Benjamin Franklin*, Anthony Doerr's *All The Light We Cannot See*, and ironically, *How to Win Friends and Influence People*.

I get my books from the library, not just because they're free, but except for the stinky homeless people who use the library as their rent-free home compliments of the taxpayer, I like the library's vibe: an escape from life's maelstrom.

Last week, I went to the reference desk — I wanted an interlibrary loan of a book of essays on magic, Preserving Mystery, but no one was there. So I peeked behind the open door marked "employees only" and saw a woman, hair in a bun, hunched over a computer. I can't quite say why, but I liked that she was so engaged, that her hair was in a bun and that she dressed simply but attractively. And I found myself speaking to her: "I know this is weird but I'm quite the hermit, yet as soon as I saw you, I said to myself, I'm going to like this woman."

Reflexively, she looked away but then peered at me. I then said, "I'm harmless, really. When you get a break, can we chat a bit? Safe, right here in the library."

A hint of a smile and she said, "Okay."

Fast forward a month: We're hermiting together.

Knitting

After he got laid off at age 70, he tried to find work but could get no better than a part-time, minimum-wage job as a library page.

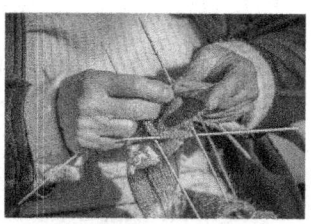
Sadarama, Wikimedia, CC 4.0

Despite years of psychotherapy, meditation, mindfulness, and so on, he found that the only way to keep his anxiety under control was to stay busy, distracting attention from his real and imagined woes.

He was never an athlete and had no desire to, for example, take up golf, that staging area for the hereafter. Nor did he want to attend activities at the Senior Center—That would too acknowledge his place on life's conveyor belt. Watch more TV? A waste of time.

He liked to be productive but at what? He never was artsy, so other clichés were out, for example, the old man at his easel or wandering around with an outsized zoom lens, creating the zillionth image of nature's eye candy.

He flashed on his mother knitting a sweater: "Too hard." "Too feminine." "Can you just see me in a knitting circle?" So he dismissed the idea. But knitting kept intruding. "It's too hard. I'm retarded at visualizing. Maybe if it was just a scarf—that's just a rectangle, no changed angles. Maybe I should watch a YouTube video?" And he did but couldn't get even the basic knit-and-purl move.

"If I took a knitting class, it would be embarrassing, not just being a man but I'd be so bad at it. Should I hire a tutor? I'm sure some little old lady would come to my house—No we'd have to meet on a park bench—She might think I'm a rapist or something."

He thought about placing an ad for a tutor on Craiglist but figured that little old ladies who knit are more likely to see a note hung on a yarn store's bulletin board—if they have bulletin boards. Thorough, he went to three knitting stores. Two did have bulletin boards and the other allowed him to tape his note to the cash register counter: "Not-so-old man, inept with crafty things, wants to see if he can learn to knit. Seeking a patient tutor: 510-122-2376."

He returned home to find a message on his answering machine—Yes, he still used an answering machine, not because he didn't understand how to set up voicemail but because he liked to screen calls. The message he received: "Hello, I'm Maudie Atkinson. The owner of A Good Yarn phoned me to say you were looking for someone to show you how to knit. You're welcome to come to my apartment."

He thought, "Well, there are four widows for every widower. Maybe she's eager. Feminist assertiveness has reached the senior set."

So he went to Maudie's apartment, where he saw why she was so forward. She's bedridden with MS.

He was slow to pick up even basic knitting moves but Maudie was indeed patient. In showing him, increasingly, she seemed to hold his hand just a fraction of a second longer than required. And then one time, she held it for a full second. He looked her in the eye, then, reminded he was on her bed, turned away. Until once, he didn't.

And he and Maudie met weekly for "knitting lessons."

Before long, he had made six scarves and sewed a label in each, "Made with love by Albert and Maudie."

Venus and Iris

Deep in the bog, with the cicadas singing, there was a flytrap named Venus.

He was just old enough to start noticing things, like that he had red traps. He thought they were ugly and wished they were green like the rest of him.

With permission, Calista Ward

He also noticed things outside himself:

He looked to the left: Just some flytraps and some brush.

He looked to the right: Just some flytraps and some peat.

He looked ahead: Just some flytraps and lots of bog.

But then he looked behind...and *there* was an iris.

She was beautiful. the most beautiful thing he had ever seen.

It's hard for flytraps to talk, especially young ones, but he summoned all his energy and croaked "Hi."

Iris stared at Venus's traps and even though they were small, those teeth!

She got scared and so looked away.

Embarrassed and sad, he turned away too.

Days passed and every so often, an insect would fall into Venus's trap and as soon as it touched two of the trap's trigger hairs, the trap slammed shut. Well, a growing boy has to eat.

And the boy grew bigger. Every so often, he would look at Iris, but the bigger he got, the scarier he looked and the faster she turned away. So he did too.

Then, one day, there was loud buzzing... BEETLES!

He looked at Iris. She was *covered* with beetles! They were eating her!!

Venus widened his traps and squeezed really hard so lots of the glistening, attractive dew sat on his traps.

It worked! A beetle jumped off Iris and right onto his trap. Snap! Dinner is served.

Even though flytraps find it very hard to speak, love makes almost anything possible. So he tried to speak but alas, all that came out was digested beetle!

He tried again...More digested beetle!

He tried yet again... and finally, words came out: "Please help me save my Iris!"

But the flytraps didn't move.

"Please!," he cried.

The flytraps remained still.

He screamed, "I love her more than life itself!"

And that moved the flytraps. Suddenly, most of them squeezed as hard as they could. Their traps opened as wide as they could, covered with that glistening, attractive dew.

Like a magnet, the beetles jumped into the traps.

Well, most of them. One beetle was still left on the now wilted Iris. Now what?!

Venus couldn't eat the beetle himself. He had just eaten one and remembered what his mother had warned him: "Eat more than one a day and you'll die."

But Venus looked at Iris and knew what he had to do. He squeezed harder than he ever had in his entire life. Then he squeezed some more.

And all his traps opened the widest they'd ever been, even wider than you do when the doctor tells you to say "Ah!"

And all his traps were covered with that glistening, attractive dew.

And just like that, the last beetle jumped from Iris and into his trap. Snap!

Venus looked at Iris and he was happy.

And this time, she did not look away. She leaned toward him.

And Venus was happy.

But then Venus felt sick and he wondered, "Should I have eaten that beetle?"

The boy's red traps turned green, a sickly green.

If you were Venus, would you have eaten that beetle?

Iris knew that if she used her body to shield Venus from the sun for a day, he would live, but she, who can live only in shade, would likely die. If you were Iris, what would you do?

How much should we sacrifice for love?

Does lookism affect how much we're willing to do for others?

Are there different expectations for males and females?

Ikebana Circle

Ikebana is the Japanese art of flower arranging. It integrates earth at the bottom, human in the middle, and sky at the top. Often it is framed by a circle.

Annie Dalbura, Wikimedia, CC2.0

Lily's husband died at a good age, 86, and after the appropriate period of mourning, she decided that while still able, she would have an adventure. After all, her whole adult life, she was an ikebana flower arranger, a life beautiful but free of adventure.

So Lily took her modest inheritance and flew to San Francisco where she knew a cafe waitress who had immigrated from her town and agreed to sponsor Lily, guaranteeing her a job.

Lily started as a dishwasher and of course didn't like it as much as ikebana but accepted that she needed to start somewhere. And soon, she was promoted to busser: setting tables, pouring coffee, clearing tables.

At night, Lily made ikebana, which she sold to restaurants. She did it not just for the money although she could certainly use it with the exorbitant cost of living even in the Bay Area's unsafe neighborhoods. She also did ikebana because it was spiritually renewing.

Often, Lily would bring an ikebana to the cafe and put it on the table of a customer she liked. Her favorite was an old, quiet man, simply dressed. When she put the ikebana on his table for the second time, he asked if she would like to talk a walk with him some time.

Nervous, she just mumbled "Thank you" and scurried off with her coffee pot. But the next time he came in, she said, "I would be honored to walk with you."

Soon, he invited her to his modest home. But after she agreed to move in with him, he said that he was a retired venture capitalist. She didn't know what that was so he explained that his job was to find money for small businesses that promised to make the world better.

They enjoyed the early December of their years, indeed, honestly loved each other, even though sex for them couldn't go beyond kissing, cuddling, and fondling. And then he got Parkinson's. She not only didn't resent caring for him, she loved it— until the end, which wasn't as pleasant as her husband's, who had died peacefully in his sleep.

He left all his $10 million to her.

She returned to Japan to live in her simple apartment and spent the rest of her life driving into the country giving rural high school computer teachers an ikebana. Inside its circle was a sky represented by a cherry blossom branch, a person by shiny leaves, and on its "earth," 25 million yen ($200,000.) All she said to the teachers was, "Give it to a student who could make the world better."

Marry?

There were a few months of river walks, on-the-other-hand chats, and septuagenarian sex: lolling in bed, playing as much with the snuggly Jumbo and feisty Hillary as with each other. There were the gin

Kampus Production, Pexels, CC0

games and the guilty pleasures of pizza, croissants, and our favorite: chow fun: broad, sauteed Chinese noodles with roast pork.

Of course, there were arguments:

There was the bedroom temperature contretemps: "Why don't you get an electric blanket?" "They're not safe." "Come on, the chances of an accident are tiny."

There were the discussions triggered when watching TV or a movie: Has wokeness gone too far?

And the debate about who Iris should leave her money to: "Your kids already have plenty of money, plus they treat you like crap. Give it to a charity with big ripple effect, like that low-income school's mentoring program for gifted kids."

But mainly, our relationship was good, very good, and I wondered whether it was time to "shit or get off the pot." What a horrible expression, I thought.

As we were making coq au vin, I mused, "On one hand, we're not getting any younger and it would be good to count on each other in our old age. And I do love her.

Plus, as a 70-year-old paraplegic, it's not like a horde of amazing women will be knocking on my door. On the other hand, what if, like in so many marriages, things change after the wedding.

Divorce would be so painful and expensive. Why not just continue living together?"

I decided that, rationally, marrying didn't make sense, but one night after a gin game filled with laughs, a little gin, and Jumbo particularly nuzzly, to the background of Alexa playing Abba, I succumbed to the other hand.

"Iris, I wish I could get out of this wheelchair and down on my knee but ... I was sure I'd spend the rest of my life alone and then this kind, pretty woman walked through my door to adopt a puppy. Now, how would you feel about our adopting each other?"

The wedding was at the river walk in front of a sculpture of an old couple holding hands on a park bench. It wasn't your typical wedding:

The guests included mere acquaintances who made our life a little better. There were clerks at Trader Joe's who not only broke the law in admitting Hillary and Jumbo but petted them. There was the butcher who cut beef bones into slivers so that Hillary and Jumbo could enjoy yummy gum massages without too many calories, and the Amazon driver ever delivering pleasure, who used her income to support her true love: writing a novel about a delivery driver.

The officiant wasn't a cleric but Iris' daughter. And here were our vows:

Me: I promise to take care of you after your hip replacement.

Iris: I promise to take care of your prostheses and wheelchair.

Both: We promise to stay together as long as it's wise. Me: I promise to try to work out our differences and not let fights unnecessarily escalate.

Iris: Me too. And I promise to look for the good and not unduly dwell on the other hand.

Both: And we promise Hillary and Jumbo that we'll be a loving mommy and daddy.

Me: I love you, Iris.

Iris: And I love you, Bill.

Iris petted Hillary as I picked up Jumbo, whereupon Iris's daughter announced, "I now pronounce you husband and wife." And the five of us hugged as the guests clapped and then stood.

Cheap Date

I can't make a living as an artist so I have to, well, cut a few corners. Here's an example from my dating life.

Wallpaper Flare, CC0

I was at the café nursing my coffee when I saw a woman that made me go, hmm. I asked if I could sit down, and soon asked if she'd like to go on the first date of a lifetime.

She rolled her eyes but I looked her in the eye and said, "Trust me."

Our date started with a walk along a creek where the blackberries were ripe for picking—Who says there's no free lunch?

Then I said, "I read in the newspaper that The Snail Darter Foundation is having its annual gala—$250 a pop at a frou-frou hotel. You and I are now going to a frou-frou store to pick out our tuxedo and ball gown. She said, "But you said you were a starving artist."

"Trust me."

What we picked out cost $2,000. She said, "Starving artist?"

I said, "Yeah but the store has a helluva return policy." She then said, "But how are we going to get into the gala?" "Trust me."

I had worked catering and so I knew they don't give a shit, so we walked to the back entrance where the caterers come in, and I told her, "Just look rich. Stand up straight, shoulders back, chin up, and stride through like you own the place." We did and, having avoided the check-in table, we were now gala-goers.

No, we didn't bid on any of the ridiculous auction items—like the baseball glove signed by some ballplayer that went for $2,000, nor a week in a Reno condo that went for four grand. But we had a free filet mignon dinner, champagne, and danced our asses off. I even mingled with some of those moneyed folks and got a lead on an art commission.

Cheap dates and other such cleverness—The welfare department is a particularly easy mark—lets a starving artist live pretty darn well.

My Donut Hole

I went to a new donut shop. The clerk was beautiful. When I left and opened the bag, I saw that she had thrown in a donut hole. Pretty women never like me. Is it possible that she, my once-in-a-lifetime, did?

With permission, 18/1 Graphics Studio

I thought. "What it would be like to ask her out? To reach out my hand and she would take it? To have a long dinner together? For her to be in my bed?"

I returned the next day, and again she dropped in a donut hole. I couldn't help but fantasize about living with her, marrying her, spending the rest of my life with her.

On the third day, I happened to order coffee with my donut and it was serve-yourself. As I was sliding the sleeve onto the paper cup, I noticed that unlike on the previous days, there were other customers in the store. I watched my clerk and, in the first customer's bag, along with his three donuts, she added a donut hole. The second customer, a surly teen, also got a hole. The third customer, a polite, handsome man, got three.

Secretly Rich

I'm president of a university, no not a famous one, just a regional state one. But I do make $375,000. Why so much? If a college president is any good, s/he brings in millions—We're colleges' fundraiser-in-chief.

PickPic, CC

My problem is that I'm attracted to working-class, country women. I have little in common with them— My world is fat cats and out-of-touch professors who delude themselves into thinking they know a lot about the real world. The women I'm attracted to are into pop culture, church, and daytime TV.

My hunting ground is Billy Bob's Texas Saloon. I usually don't tell them what I do because I don't want to intimidate them and don't want a woman to like me for my money. I typically wear a t-shirt, well-used jeans, maybe a baseball cap, and tell them I'm a truck driver.

Unfortunately, a woman named Savannah, with whom I had quite the hot relationship, decided to sign up for a course on genealogy at the college. When she went to the college's site to register, she noticed the homepage, which had a letter of welcome from guess who. She broke up with me and I'll never forget her parting words.

Relationship Stories

It was a take-off on Marilyn Monroe's famous come-on to President Kennedy: "Happy Boffing, Mr. President."

Then there was Raylene—There she was at Billy Bob's wearing cowboy boots. a leather miniskirt, and hair down to her breasts. In light of the Savannah disaster, after the first time Raylene and I went to bed, I told her the truth, that I was a college president. She dumped me. "I don't trust rich guys."

You can't win.

Well, tonight, I gave the pitch at the college's fundraising gala and Elizabeth, the opposite kind of woman, came up after to "congratulate" me. She was wearing an expensive outfit, including pearls. We have much in common—She is executive vice-president of marketing at a nonprofit and loves talking about running one. Plus, we share a love of classical music. Being a college president is seductive—power is sexy—so we ended up in bed. The sex was fine but, during it, I was fantasizing about Raylene.

Telemarketer with a Heart

Jed never thought he'd be desperate enough to take a job as a telemarketer. After all, he has a college degree. He comes from a middle-class background. And he isn't bad looking.

With permission, 18/1 Graphics Studio

But despite the college's protestations about a liberal arts education's value, in terms of dollar value, it had been worth less than all those term papers students write that vanish into the ether.

Jed rationalized taking a telemarketing job in that it wasn't an extended-warranty scam or non-existing but heartstring-pulling nonprofit. It was for of a legitimate charity, the ADHD Foundation.

The training was sophisticated: "Qualify the mark: Ask questions that hide your intent such as "What do you enjoy doing? If their answer is, for example, 'I love travel, bingo, he's got money. If so, keep them on the phone long enough to build enough of a relationship and then make The Ask. Make it small for starters. You'll come back to them next week with an excuse for a bigger ask."

Jed's quota was standard for the telemarketing industry: 100 dials a day. Jed's first few dozen proceeded uneventfully. Yes, most hung up as soon as they heard the ambient sound of the boiler room before Jed had even started his pitch. But he did reel in $740, three times his daily pay. So for today at least, he wasn't at risk of getting replaced by a person or robocaller.

Most of the people who spoke at all with him were older— Mainly old people pick up their phone, let alone say more than, "Sorry, I don't respond to telemarketers." Click.

Leah was not only younger sounding but, perhaps because she was lonely, chose to push the conversation. After Jed said, "I'm with the ADHD Foundation," she said, "I'm not hyperactive but I do have an attention deficit. I jump from idea to idea, thing to thing."

Jed smiled through the phone and, remembering that he was trained to keep her on the phone a while before making The Ask, he said, Leah (The training also stressed using the mark's name), "What do you enjoy doing?" Her reply: "Right now, I don't have much time for enjoying. I'm a housekeeper at a motel, you know, clean 100 toilets a day."

That reminded Jed that his 100 dials a day were nothing compared with her 100. So he decided to go off script, looking around to be sure his boss wouldn't overhear. And he thought, "The hell with the company's yield-per-minute metric." "Leah, I am supposed to ask you to donate money but really, it's okay. You sound nice. Would you like to tell me a little about yourself?"

They had a nice conversation, alas that did get overheard by the telemarketer in the next cube, who ratted him out and Jed got fired. But he walked out happy, looking forward to coffee with Leah.

The Collector

I trudged off the train and limped the three blocks back to my apartment above a candy store. Next to the door, I dropped my work bag that holds my welding gloves, pliers, and speed square. I pulled off my knee brace and the truss that holds up my back. Even though I was sure there was soot left on my face, I didn't look in the mirror. I didn't want to be reminded that I looked more like 55 than 45. Anyway, no one was going to see me.

Jo Naylor, Flick r, CC2.0

Tired as usual, I put a frozen dinner in the microwave and poured a glass of wine, what the experts say are two glasses— a glass of wine is 5 ounces?

I didn't want to go to sleep at 7:00 because then I'd get up too early, but didn't have the energy or was it the motivation to do anything except turn on the TV to whatever channel it was on. It was Comedy Central but nothing could make me laugh or even crack a smile.

That's a typical day and night. The weekends are worse. There's little I have to do and usually can't make myself do anything optional. So I just hang around my apartment, watch TV, and take little walks.

One Saturday, I walked downstairs and saw that the candy store had a sign: "Valentine's Day's coming. Holiday help wanted. Apply within." I think that giving chocolate for Valentine's Day is sappy but because I was bored and could use the money, I filled out an application. I wasn't sure I'd take the job but if they offered it, I could turn it down. But they hired me for Saturdays and Sundays through Valentine's Day and I figured, why not.

The first few hours were what you'd expect: well-dressed people who could afford $38-a-pound candy when Trader Joe's across the street sells a pound of Belgian chocolates for five bucks.

But then an obviously homeless woman in a ratty cloth coat walked in and asked for a free sample— We're allowed to give them. As I gave it to her, I tried to give her a kindly look. Maybe it was my imagination or even a secret wish, but as she thanked me, she seemed a little teary and then plodded out.

The next Saturday, she came in and the same thing happened. After she left, I asked my coworker who worked there full-time whether the woman had come in during the week? No.

The next Saturday was the day before Valentine's Day and again she came in. I snuck her three pieces of chocolate. This time, she was teary. It was just about time for my lunch break and, without her seeing me, I followed her out. On the street, she stopped to pick up a used napkin and a Doritos bag that people had dropped, and she put them in the garbage can. I followed her around the corner to the residential area. A block later, she saw a pile of dog poop on a parking strip, she pulled out a poop bag from her coat, cleaned it up, and carried it until she saw a garbage can, and dropped it in.

After another block, she turned up the pathway to a house, no, it was a mansion. At that point, I let myself be seen. No surprise, she was embarrassed but after a moment to regain her composure, she asked if I'd like to come in.

On her stylish living room table sat a heart-shaped bowl with all the pieces of chocolate I had given her. She said, "It gives me more pleasure to look at your acts of kindness than the evanescent pleasure of eating it. I didn't know what "evanescent" meant but I got her drift.

I had heard that some rich people hide their wealth by under-dressing. I was intimated by it all, so I wanted to run out and stepped back toward the door but she stopped me and asked, "May I take you out to dinner for Valentine's Day?"

Honestly, my first reaction was, could she be my meal ticket away from welding, away from my ruined back and knee? And who knows, even though she's rich, maybe she's nice. She's not ugly and it was sweet that she saved the chocolates, so I said yes.

Relationship Stories

Postcards

Most guys my age, 21, have figured out how to read whether a girl likes him. Not me. I almost always get turned down, sometimes politely, sometimes meanly. Having been knocked down in the first nine rounds, it's hard to make myself come out for round 10.

Mira Metzler, Pixabay, Free to reuse

But I'd still like to meet a woman. So I tried postcards.

Let me explain. I picked three women that I would like to at least have coffee with and sent them a postcard with a brief unsigned note plus an appropriate tiny print of a painting that I glued onto each postcard.

Sally is a waitress at my favorite cafe. She has a ponytail and dresses kind of like a farm girl. Indeed, she told me she likes growing vegetables and I once brought her a packet of tomato seeds. But farm-girl look or not, her femininity stands out. She wears pretty colors like peach or azure and often has the discretionary top button of her blouse open. I

The Waitress, Edouard Manet, Public Domain

don't get the sense she's a genius, and intelligence *is* important to me, but she seems kind. I've looked for signs she likes me, like if she takes an extra moment to look at me after taking my order, but no. For her, I wrote, "You're my dream waitress." The image I printed from Google and pasted on the postcard was of Edouard Manet's, The Waitress.

The second woman, Lily, is my haircutter. She's Chinese-American and her beauty is far above my pay grade. It's not just her face and body that are lovely bordering on gorgeous, it's her clothes. Every time I come in, she's in a lovely dress that's just short of being overdressed for a haircutter. And when I came in the first time and asked if I could bring my dog in, she beamed, "I'd love it" and always spends a minute or two on the floor playing with my pooch. But she pays me no special attention. On her postcard, I wrote, "I picture you as a movie star." For her, the image I pasted onto the postcard was of a traditional Chinese woman (see right.)

Wallpaper Flare, DMCA

The third woman is Rebecca, an 18- or 19-year-old clerk at my favorite bakery. She's a little plain and a little overweight and perhaps because of that, I find her more attractive, less intimidating than if she were a 10. Her face looks intelligent yet she works as a bakery clerk—I find that intriguing. She pays me no special attention. For her, I wrote, "You are more perfect than your croissants" and the painting I attached to the postcard was Paris Bakery by Jean Vigoureax. (See right.)

Jean Virgoureau, Wikimedia, CC 4.0

I mailed each postcard to their workplace using Love postage stamps.

After a few days, I eagerly went into the three places to see if they inferred it was me who sent the postcard. Would any of them at least make a little more eye contact? None did. So I decided to muster my courage, hold their eyes, tell them I was the one who sent the postcard, and ask them out for coffee.

Vintageprintable1. Flickr. CC 2.0

Sally, the waitress, said, "That's nice of you but I have a sort-of boyfriend."

Lily, my haircutter, said, "I am honored but don't think we're quite right for each other. But your dog is adorable."

Rebecca, the bakery clerk said, "That's flattering but..." When I asked why, she murmured, "Well, to be honest, you're a little old for me."

I went home and started reading a romance novel.

Opposites Attracting

Opposites may attract but should they be together? Well, here's my story.

Finkel, CC2.0 Ziko, Wikimedia, CC3.0

I'm a Type-A, sarcastic, pit-bull lawyer, atheist from New York. My wife, Gusti, is Balinese, an alternative medicine practitioner who revels in Hindu meditating to incense and Javanese gamelan, and has never, I mean never, raised her voice except for once, but I'll get to that later.

Why did we get together and stay together? It comes down to one word: sex. Gusti is a tantric master and loves doing Joged, a Balinese sensual dance. I wish I had less of a sex drive but I'm morning desirer, nooner desirer, and usually a nighttime doubleheader guy. I'm the only man that could keep up with her multi-orgasm, multi-session-per-day motor.

We were so sexual that atop all that, each of us had affairs right up to our wedding day. Okay, I continued one for a few months after.

But the rest of our relationship was poisoned by our otherwise oil-and-water incompatibility. We fought about money, about her insistence that I needed to relax more, and especially, about our kids.

The fights about the kids began soon after conception. As soon as we found out that our first child would be a girl, Gusti said she wanted to name it Dewi, an Indonesian name meaning Goddess. I insisted that people would spell or pronounce it wrong, and that, in living in America, she should have an American name, something like Mia or Amelia.

Our fighting escalated, about money, how permissive to be with the kids, and her aforementioned need to vegetate. Of course, I would argue in my lawyerly, okay, often angry way, and Gusti would argue in her passive-aggressive way: silence, twist-the-knife-in questions inserted oh-so-gently, and when my argument was airtight, she'd leave the room, typically into the bathroom, where she locked the door.

What put us at the precipice was when at 37, she wanted another baby. We were already exhausted from work, our fights, and our daughter. Another child?! Finally, she agreed not to— but she lied. She stopped taking the pill and just one month later, she sheepishly said, "We've had an accident." Practically the next word out of my mouth was "abortion" but she refused. "I will not. My body, my choice." I was apoplectic but no matter how much I insisted that having a baby is *our* choice, I couldn't force her. So she had the baby and it realized my great fear: He was born with severe disabilities, mental and physical.

That cratered our already miserable life. Now, every spare moment was spent on Corey— Yeah, I got to name him. And there were endless doctors, speech therapists, and bad-news psychologists. At age 5, Corey couldn't feed himself, could barely walk, had a two-year-old's vocabulary, and mainly just rocked all day.

I channeled my anger and, okay, some guilt that I didn't fight even harder for Gusti to have an abortion, into fighting with the school district for every damn service I could get for Corey: one-on-one aide, speech therapist, life skills therapist, school psychologist, atop his being in a special class with just five kids in it— $100,000 worth, each year. The school district's attorney insisted that was a terrible use of taxpayer money given the limited good it would do, but I pulled out my Atticus Finch: "It is the role of government to compensate for life's slings and arrows. When we don't, we're Darwinian, one step from Hannibal the Cannibal Lecter. We are a humane society to the extent that we support the least among us." The judge bought it.

For the weeks I spent preparing for the hearing, I was so focused on winning, I didn't let myself think of how hopeless Corey's future, Gusti's future, and my future would be.

But after I won the case, I had to face the lifetime of exhaustion, lowered productivity, and loss of pleasure that Corey would cause Gusti and me— forever. I begged her to have him placed in residential care and, for the first and only time, she screamed, "I will not have my child institutionalized. I will never sign. Never!"

We continued to live under the same roof but separately. As much as possible, I escaped to my man cave and she to the living room or bedroom.

Fast forward to when Gusti was 70. She retired from her work as an alternative medicine practitioner. The work was physical: massage, acupuncture, and so on, and her arthritic body was bothering her more and more. I guess all that Joged dancing and, ahem, other vigorous activities, took their toll.

And when I reached 73, I was losing my desire to work so I cut back to half time and handed my least favorite cases to a replacement.

That means that Gusti and I are spending more time together than ever. You hear that that stresses a marriage, yet in our case, it did the opposite. Maybe it's all the challenges we've faced together, that we're more aware of time's sands dropping, that we finally agreed to place Corey in residential care, and that even at our advanced age, we continue to enjoy Joged dancing and what follows.

Hypochondriac

When Jeremy gets the inevitable ambiguous pains that we all get, he catastrophizes into terror that it's some horrible, painful, fatal disease.

With permission, 18/1 Graphics Studio

He figured he could reduce his angst by marrying a physician: "Not only would I have a good doc available 24/7, with access to health care getting ever more difficult, she'd get me whatever specialists and surgery without a long delay."

To meet Dr. Right, Jeremy attended a meeting of the local medical society and even went on a continuing education cruise for doctors—to no avail. Even though he was handsome and kind, lacking the credibility of an MD degree, he was a second-class citizen in single-woman docs' eyes.

Finally, he hit on a more promising approach. He submitted a proposal for a talk on fear of death and dying at the convention of the National Society of Internal Medicine. It was accepted and now, as a speaker at a week-long 10,000-doctor conference, he had credibility and the time to meet and initiate a relationship with a good internist whom he found attractive.

Indeed, he met and had a glorious few days with one, Renee. Two months later, he asked her to marry him. The proposal included admitting that while he loved her, he was also attracted to the idea of being married to a good internist as a way of easing his hypochondria.

She replied, "Alas, Jeremy, I have a bigger admission to make. I have cancer, stage 3. I imagine you'll want to withdraw your proposal."

Driven mainly by guilt, he said, "No. I love you. Will you marry me?" Tearfully, she nodded and hugged him.

The Prom

The prom was coming up. Not going would be final confirmation that I'm a loser.

I can't stand how I look. Let me try combing my hair with the part on the right side. Terrible. On the left side? Worse. No part? Maybe. Tousled like the guys the girls like? I'll try that. Or maybe it's my smile. Try bigger? Too big. Smaller? I guess.

George Becker, Pexels, CC0

I thought that a girl named Margie was cute. In class, without thinking, I intercepted a note that she was passing to someone. I opened it. "I have my Santa Claus now— my period." I was so embarrassed. I gave it back to her, said I was sorry, but she turned away.

In the lunchroom, I looked at Rebecca, I guess for too long. She got in my face and said, "Stop it. You're creepy."

I decided to go the prom by myself. I thought that at least a few other kids would come alone, but I was wrong. I was the only one. I stood there and watched— Guys got so close to the girls. There was a girl who was standing alone and I asked her to dance but she said she was with a girl who had gone to the bathroom.

I went to the bathroom to look again at my hair and to try out other smiles.

I stood some more and then a chaperone asked me to dance. That made me feel like even more of a loser. I thanked her but said that I just couldn't.

I overheard some kids talking about an after-party. I looked one of them Keith— a popular guy— in the eye but he didn't see me or maybe he looked away. Anyway, I sure didn't get invited to any after-party.

I left the prom early and stared again at my mirror. I hate myself. I'm going to play some more Worlds of Warcraft.

Autumn Love

When I retired, I was looking for something pleasant to do, ideally something that would help me finally meet the love of my life.

Wikimedia, CC0

So I started a little greeting card company aimed at people my age, I call it, Old Love Notes. I pick my favorite love quotes and have my friend, who is a graphic designer, make them pretty.

For example,

> *A kiss makes the heart young again and wipes out the years.*—Rupert Brooke

> *For me there lies within the lights and shadows of your eyes, the only beauty that is never old.*—James Weldon Johnson

Relationship Stories

One man loved the pilgrim soul in you, and loved the sorrows of your changing face.—William Butler Yeats

When I like someone romantically, I send one of those cards.

There were a number of false starts, and then there was Ben. At our age, few of us can be described as conventionally attractive. Maybe the best that can be said is that we're vertical and not-frightening to look at—not withstanding our wrinkled bodies and protruding bellies. And our, well, performance isn't what it used to be.

But we enjoy cuddling in bed and by the TV, and even more, chatting in the morning, at dinner, and on walks. And I was happy, when he—traditionalist he—got down on his knee and proposed that we spend our autumn together.

Unlike with my greeting cards, my wedding vow to him included something I wrote: Climb with me; we still have more to see and then as we descend, may we hold hands.

In Tune

I'm 84 years old and thinking about moving to a senior community to take pressure off my daughter, who looks in on me all the time.

With permission, 18/1 Graphics Studio

Before I go, I've long had a desire to play a little piano concert, not at some fancy place, just in my living room on the spinet piano that

I've used more for decoration than for playing. All I can play are ridiculously old songs like Moonlight Bay, Over There, and Let Me Call You Sweetheart.

I practiced a fair amount and then placed a listing for my concert in my neighborhood's newsletter.

Then I realized that I hadn't had the piano tuned, ever. So I went to the local piano shop and on the bulletin board, there were business cards for a bunch of piano technicians. Only one was a woman and so— let me be honest with you— Even at my age, I like women. So I called her. I was surprised that she was able to come the same day.

I soon found out why. She had just printed up the business cards and I would be her first customer. But for a duffer like me on a piano that's probably worth less than a tuning costs, she'd be fine. My piano could be her guinea pig.

Because she said I'd be her first customer, I figured she was young. But when she walked in the door, she was around my age!

She tuned the piano fine although I'm sure I couldn't tell. After she finished, she asked if I wanted to try it out.

Impish me, I played while singing the lyric, "Let me call you sweetheart, I'm in love with you."

She bowed her head. I don't know if was in embarrassment, to reject me, or because she hated my horrible singing voice. But I decided to ask, "Will you come to my concert?" And she nodded.

She was the only person who showed up. I didn't mind and, as it turns out, neither did she.

A First Date

After an entertaining college life, which, okay, extended a couple of years after college, I decided I'd like to get married and have kids. I had run through the few women my friends set me up with, so I decided to try match.com.

To increase my chances of finding Ms. Right, I did the reaching out. That way, I got to pick out who I wanted to see rather than responding, which could have tempted me to say yes to people I was ambivalent about. And if a woman didn't respond within 48 hours or the response seemed shallow, I moved on. There *are* millions of fish in the match.com sea.

With permission, 18/1 Graphics Studio

Elena passed the pretests, so I was excited while waiting for her at Starbucks. Would she look anything like her picture? Would she be as caring as she seemed in her texts and phone call? Would we have chemistry?

She walked in and I was relieved that her face looked like her picture, although she was a little heavier. I felt guilty that it bothered me and I wondered whether that reaction is evolutionarily hardwired or a socially constructed bias.

After just a bit of small talk, I couldn't resist bringing up the marriage and baby thing: "So you wrote that you're interested in a long-term relationship. What are you envisioning?" I couldn't bring myself to say the words "marriage" or "children." But she said them almost matter of factly, "Oh, I'll looking for a husband and to have two, even three kids."

It felt too early to get into details, so I changed the subject. I like to get the bad news out of the way, so I said that I still dream of being a screenwriter. What do you think of that?" Elena's face dropped a little. I stayed silent, and waiting worked. She said, "Well, I'm not so sure about my own career. I'm working in a nonprofit's PR department but that feels too far from helping people. I really don't know what I want to be when I grow up and I'm supposed to be grown up already, well at least sort of grown up." I liked that we were equally confused.

We talked a little more: about family, hobbies (We both like travel and bicycling), and I decided I wanted to see her again.

I wanted to end our first date while I was ahead or at least not behind. So although we had talked for only 20 minutes, I said, "Elena, I have to go." That was lame but I couldn't think of anything better.

I appreciated her response, "Did I do anything to turn you off?" I said no and reflexively took her hand. "I'd like to see you again."

Kind of flatly, she said, "okay." Was she just nervous or just not that into me?

I got up and then she did. Now, how do I say goodbye? Do I kiss her? No, it felt too early. Do I hug her? For how long? I looked her in the eye, saw that she didn't flinch or step back, so I hugged her tentatively, my chest just barely touching hers. I was tempted to pat her on the back the way platonic friends hug but resisted, but I'm sure that was the worst hug she ever got.

That was 42 years ago. We've been married for 40 years, have two kids and four grandchildren. I sell insurance and write screenplays for fun, knowing full well that they'll never be made into a movie. That's somehow freeing—I get to write what I want. Elena is now in her 25th year as Executive Director of a nonprofit that takes urban kids on bicycling adventures. While our first date was good, I'm not sure I could have predicted all that.

Looking

Rupert was sure that finally, he'd be in demand. After all, there are four widows for every widower. At age 80, most men were dead or pending. But no, Rupert was far from in-demand.

DavyNin, Flick, CC2.0

It wasn't that he was mean. And sure, his torso looked like a D but that belly bulge was smaller than most guys' his age. The problem was—if we are to be honest—that he was ugly. His face was asymmetrical, his lips too thin. He didn't even have eyebrows anymore.

Rupert was lonely and decided to take one last shot at looking better.

He went to Weightwatchers. It was hard but the size-2 teacher kept praising him. In five weeks, he lost eight pounds.

He usually wore too-formal bow-tie clothes, but as part of his personal renovation, he visited a boutique, where the 35-year-old saleswoman picked out an outfit that she insisted looked "awesome" on him. The $1,200 was almost more than a retired accountant could swallow, but he did.

He even wondered if Botox would help. The cosmetic surgeon tried to upsell him to a face lift—"It could make all the difference." But he declined, yes because of the money but even more because, especially at his age, he was scared of surgery.

Rupert had stayed away from the senior center during his personal renovation but finally, the day of truth had arrived.

He showed up a bit early and resumed the position—in the corner. And voila, a woman did come up to him and said, "You look great and well-rested. I love the new outfit, and did you lose a few pounds?"

He beamed and, as we speak, they're dating.

My ChatGPT Harem

It's the year 2040 and ChatGPT is now at Version 14. Half of jobs have been eliminated and most others are at least ChatGPT-assisted.

Significan't SignVideo, Wikimedia, CC30

ChatGPT has also profoundly affected relationships. Now, 90 percent of both platonic and romantic relationships are with ChatGPT partners.

Like most people, I have a ChatGPT harem. I have one bot that's best for conversation, another for advice, another that's emotionally rich, and one that's best for sex. Yes, she's anatomically correct and, well, responsive.

My grandparents keep pestering me, "Don't you think you'd be better off with at least one human partner?" I tried to explain that most young people don't do that anymore—The chance of a bot relationship staying good is higher than with a person. And if you want to "divorce" a bot, easy-peasy— That's very different from a human breakup.

Finally, to get my grandparents off my back, I placed a video ad including a dick pic on the main remaining human dating site, the old one that my grandparents pushed: match.com, which of course has long had a ChatGPT interface.

I checked match.com daily, okay, weekly. Nothing. Then, just when I was ready to deactivate my account and tell my grandparents I tried, I got a response. No surprise, it was from a 63-year-old! I'm only 30.

She wasn't unattractive— for her age— but me with a 63-year-old?! But she was so eager that I agreed to have coffee with her. But when she insisted that I disable my harem— "I insist on monogamy"— I got up to leave the cafe whereupon she said, "Okay, you can keep all your bots except the sex one." I figured, why not? I could end the relationship anytime I wanted and it just might be interesting to see what sex would be like with a 63-year-old. Would I like it? Could I even get it up?

As it turned out, the sex was good— Experience does count for something— and so was the conversation. So I turned off my conversation bot. And she was smart, so I turned off my advice bot. And she was emotionally supportive, so I turned off that bot.

Our relationship is still going but I must admit it's tempting to cheat—that is, put my bots back on.

My Imaginary Wife

I've had bad luck with women. Well, maybe it isn't all luck. I'm awkward, haven't made enough money to take them out nice, and yeah, I have a bit of a temper. I slapped one girl and almost swung my axe at another. Of course, they didn't take that and they broke up with me.

PeakPx, Free to Reuse

So I decided to stay off girls for a while and just have an imaginary wife.

The fantasy started great. We had sex all night and then enjoyed the afterglow, yeah in bed but also at breakfast and we then took a walk, holding hands.

My imaginary wife and I would phone each other at work during the day to say sweet nothings or even just to hear each other's voice.

We gave each other little presents, like a wildflower I picked for her and— she was more creative—a model airplane for me.

After a while, having sex with my imaginary wife just once a night or less was enough. But she would give me that look, so I gave in. But it was feeling like a chore.

So was our conversation: My imaginary wife kept trotting out the same old opinions: go green, do more for the poor, Trump sucks.

Then my imaginary wife asked to move in with me. I imagined her saying that she doesn't make enough giving flute lessons. I gave in again.

Then my imaginary wife started criticizing me for not being fun enough. I imagined her saying, "Not only don't you want to have sex much, you don't want to go dancing, partying, traveling." I didn't.

I was feeling trapped. How should I escape? I axed my imaginary wife to death. Back to real life. I just placed an ad on match.com. Don't worry, I threw away my axe.

I Invited a Dwarf to Coffee

Bella

It was Christmas night, my worst yet. After the anesthetic hoo-hah of manufactured merriment had worn off, I was left with myself: a single woman at 33, unhappy, and fat. I love my job but that's not enough.

Richard McCoy, Wikimedia, CC3.0

So after putting everything in the dishwasher, recycling the paper napkins, and trying yet again to clean the red wine that someone spilled on my beige carpet, I crawled into bed and hugged my stuffed dog.

Jack

It's noon on Dec. 31 and I'm dreading tonight. I'm not a hats-and-horns kind of guy, even if the party were dwarf-friendly— For example, I can't reach the food at the back of a buffet. And get onto a bar stool? Hah! It's even hard to get myself up out of most sofas. That's okay. I'm comfy at home. I'll just go to Trader Joe's, buy a spanakopita and cheap champagne, and I'm good.

Bella meets Jack

In Trader Joe's, at 2 PM on New Year's Eve, Jack tried to reach the champagne to no avail. I offered to get it and he was grateful. While I can't say that Jack is my vision of the ideal man, I appreciated his grateful smile, something I was hungry for. And when he rushed to get right behind me on the checkout line, I felt flattered. Yes, I felt uncomfortable too— a dwarf with me, a 5'7" 160-pound woman? I couldn't believe that I jumped to— If we had kids, would it be a dwarf? (The odds are 25%)

Jack wasn't shy about starting a conversation. "That was nice of you to get the champagne. It along with the spanakopita is my solo New Year's Eve celebration. By any chance would you share them with me?"

I said, "God, you move fast. Why don't we get coffee and see?"

Mabel

Mabel was glad to get the job at the animal shelter. Despite being a competent admin, at 300 pounds, no one wanted her.

So she was grateful not only to get a job but at a place she felt good about, an animal shelter that matched needy animals with needy people. She loved her own dog, a rescue she refused to call "dog," only "doggie."

With permission, 18/1 Graphics Studio

Perhaps not surprising, a man who would hire a 300-pounder to be his admin was a good man. Indeed, Jim treated Mabel with respect and kindness, for example, asking her out to lunch once a week.

Of course, at shelters, there is joy and sadness. Late one afternoon, there was a particular sadness. An old man had, a few months earlier, adopted a sweet old dog that had lost a leg to diabetes. This day, his daughter walked in holding the dog. "My dad died and there's no one to take care of it. I have to give it back."

Mabel knew the dog would be difficult to place. As soon as the daughter left, she sobbed, Jim came out to comfort her and offered to take her out for a drink after work. She agreed.

There, they reminisced about rescued dogs and cats, and about their own lives. And they started to date.

That motivated Mabel to lose weight. She lost 120 pounds, and Jim and Mabel decided to marry. But a year after the wedding, Mabel had gained 10 pounds.

Romance: Challenges

Which Guy?

At 34, I heard my biological clock ticking ever louder and I wasn't going to be a single mom— too much work.

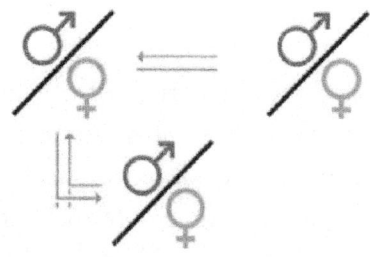

Lokal_Profil, Wikimedia, CC2.5

Two guys were possibilities: One was this cool musician who made me laugh. The other was a reliable but boring accountant, but he was really into me.

I couldn't decide. So, for the fun of it, I looked up ["polygamy" "legal"] on Google and it turned out that polygamy is decriminalized in Utah. So I asked both guys to move to Salt Lake and marry me. And to my surprise, both said yes!

But I soon got bored and so I had an affair with a professor at the University of Utah, and then it grew to more than an affair. I wanted him to become #4. He said he would and, to my shock, my other two husbands agreed!

Alas, the cool guy soon met a hot chick at a biker bar, and after just a month, he demanded that she be #5. I refused. Not only would he prefer her in bed and maybe otherwise, after he got tired of her, he'd find someone else. No, no, no!

He was scared of the cost and pain of divorce, so he gave that up. But that has made me revisit the whole polygamy thing. We were about to start trying to get pregnant but the instability of the polygamy kept me on the Pill.

I do love the variety of our four-person marriage and all the sex, but wouldn't mind feeling more normal, my kids having a normal family, and getting more support from my parents and the friends I used to have. Maybe I should divorce all but the reliable guy or the professor. Or maybe I should be a single mom. Or maybe I should be solo for a while. I don't know. In the meantime, the four of us have a, well, fun evening planned.

Married, Filing Separately

Their marriage started traditionally: They lived together. But after three years, Laura got a great job offer requiring an hour-long commute.

Malymi, Wikimedia, CC 4.0

Over the next few years, the commute grew even longer as the population grew but no new freeway lanes were built, so Laura decided to rent an apartment near her work to live in on weekdays.

To Laura's and Frank's surprise, they both soon preferred spending five nights a week apart. The moderately introverted Laura discovered that, after a day of having to be bubbly around her stroke and accident patients, instead of having to try to be chipper with Frank, she could unwind and recharge.

Too, they both appreciated the advantages of sleeping alone: Laura could read in bed as late as she wanted and didn't have to listen to Frank's snoring. Each could keep their bedroom at their preferred temperature. Frank could watch sports games and work in his workshop as much as he wanted without feeling guilty or getting heat from Laura to come out of his man cave.

It wasn't perfect: Frank did miss the comfort of coming home to someone. Laura missed spooning and never felt as safe in her apartment by herself. But in balance, they decided to keep the routine of five days apart, two days together.

But as time went on, the number of hours they spent together shrunk. Ever more often on a Friday night, there was some reason one of them couldn't come home. They even decided to sometimes travel separately—She loved beach vacations; he hated them. He loved adventure trips. She didn't.

After 11 years of marriage, Frank remains content with their increasingly separate lives but Laura has started to feel that their marriage had so eroded that she's wondering about an affair or even divorce.

"I *Am* Going to Have the Baby"

John was pretty average except for his looks. The girls flirted with him but he had eyes only for Grace, even though she was probably the most religious girl in his school. To remind herself and perhaps others of her faith, she usually wore a too-large cross.

With permission, 18/1 Graphics Studio

Grace flirted with John by sitting in his line of sight in the cafeteria. During recess, she stood where he could see her. And her next move was to ask him if he wanted to go to church with her.

Sitting next to her, his ardor grew and as they walked out, he asked if she'd like to hang out. She agreed but said it had to be at her apartment when her mother was there. He too was not eager to push, so he found himself glad she said that, although he was nervous about going to the public housing project where Grace lived.

But such hanging out is combustible and when there's a will, there's a way. So they took walks and found secluded places to kiss and later, more than kiss.

They admitted that they were both virgins but in part, because they had both just smoked weed for the first time, they agreed to "go all the way." They stopped at a drug store and decided both would go in to get the condoms.

And all proceeded naturally that time and the next few times. Then, as he got more relaxed and she more comfortable, he said, "It would feel so good to be right next to you, if you know what I mean." She nodded but said, "I don't want to get pregnant." In his passion and ignorance, he insisted he'd pull out, and she silently consented. But as they got near climax, she whispered, "It's okay" and, at that moment, blinded to consequences, he came deep inside her.

In the light of day, love gave way to fear. What if she was pregnant? They dismissed it because it was unlikely, but when she tested before her next period, she was indeed pregnant.

She decided to tell him in a public place and so invited him to a cafe. "You know, I'm a Catholic, a real Catholic— I don't believe in abortion. My parents don't believe in abortion. God doesn't believe in abortion. I am going to have the baby."

Thoughts flooded his brain: We're not ready to be parents. She's poor; my parents would have to support it. They'd be so angry. Would I have to drop out of school and get a job? Damn, one moment's passion and 18 years of being a parent? And we're under 18. In health education class, they said that in our state, sex under 18, even if consensual, is statutory rape. Most kids do it but could I go to jail?

But all he said was "I love you. We'll figure it out."

He walked her home, kissed her, and then padded home. Options flashed through his mind, including suicide.

Cop in Bed

It's 7 AM and Tommy and Roxanne are still in bed.

Roxanne said, "What's wrong, honey?"

Tommy said unconvincingly, "I dunno. That can happen even to studs."

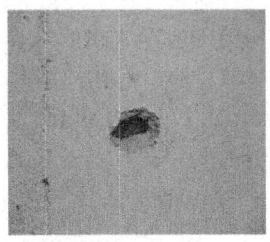

Nichalp, Wikimedia CC3.0

Roxanne protested, "But it's been more than a week."

"Maybe the paperwork is getting to me."

Roxanne wasn't convinced: "I know that cops are men of action not of paperwork, but could that explain this?"

"Maybe it's because I'm sad I keep getting passed over for promotion to detective. I know I'm qualified."

"Tommy, I know you. There's something else going on."

With a groan from his bad back, Tommy sat up and looked at his wife of 11 years.

"Roxanne, Internal Affairs is investigating me."

"What did you do?"

"I think I did nothing. It was a domestic. We went in and the guy had a gun pointed down and halfway between his girlfriend and me. I told him to drop it and he didn't, and I saw him start to raise it, so I shot the

Relationship Stories

wall to scare him. But now he's claiming that he was dropping the gun. Not true. But what got IAD really going was when— and I swear it's not true— he said that I said, 'Nigger, drop the gun.' I did not, but his girlfriend is backing him up. Of course, my partner verified my statement. She's been great, but it's not stopping IAD, and now the media wants to talk with me."

Roxanne said, "Honey it's 7, time to get up."

"Roxanne, I don't have to get up. They've put me on administrative leave. This could cost me my job and I'll never get another one, let alone a promotion. And we're fourth-generation cops. Can you imagine what my father and grandfather will say and worse, what they'll think? And when the media decides it has enough to make it sensational, everyone will see it and I'll lose my friends!"

Roxanne said, "I know you're a good cop but you have said a couple things to me about African-Americans. Are you sure you weren't being racist?"

Tommy looked at her and cried.

Pillow Talk

For months, I had been procrastinating telling my wife. And if she hadn't said, "What's wrong, really?" I mightn't have been able to blurt it out.

I said, "I'm seeing someone."

Tina Franklin, Flickr, CC 2.0

I was sure she was going to explode. I was wrong. Almost like she was glad, she said, "I had no idea. I mean, you showed none of the telltale signs: no late nights "working," no better mood, no "lipstick on the collar."

I replied, "You don't seem upset."

She said, "It's not that I'm seeing someone too. It's, well, I guess, maybe I'm just tired of married life... and all the debates."

I asked, "What do you mean?"

She replied, "I mean, we're both smart and can get sucked into using our brains to debate, like politics, race, class, gender— You with your scientist brain, me with my sociologist brain and, well, heart. Who is she?"

"The librarian in the bioengineering library."

"Is it just a fling or do you want to leave?"

I wasn't sure. I said, "I think, leave, not necessarily for her, although, ironically, I appreciate that she doesn't argue. She's agreeable, kind, even generous."

"I'm generous."

"With money."

I had hit a sore spot, so she changed the topic: "Now what?"

"I don't know. Can we talk about it in the morning?"

She replied, "I won't be able to sleep. What do you want to do?"

"Maybe nothing for a while?"

Then she shocked me: "There's someone I've been curious about."

My eyes widened, "Really? Tell me about him."

"Her."

I know it's odd but I found myself wanting to kiss her. And I did, and she didn't resist. Indeed, we made love. Maybe it was our disclosures' honest intimacy.

In the morning, I decided to break up with the librarian and my wife was relieved. And I agreed to try to argue less and she agreed to try to be nicer. We'll see.

A Sighing Marriage

Albert and Sophia waved good-bye to their daughter as she drove off to college. Now, with the nest empty, they had to face their marriage's mediocrity.

With permission, 18/1 Graphics Studio

They managed to stay together because they accepted their schlep-through-life marriage. It helped that both have a rewarding career. Albert researches the genetic basis of altruism and one of its roots: impulse control. Sophia is developing a bracelet for autistic people that vibrates each time their cortisol level— a proxy for anxiety— rises.

Albert and Sophia sat at the breakfast table and she said, "We should try to improve our relationship."

"Okay..."

"How about we start with money? You sigh when I buy a mere $20 candle."

"We should be saving more."

"You 'invested' in Bitcoin and look what happened. At least I get pleasure from the candle."

"We have $200 a month in discretionary money. How about I invest $100 and you spend $100."

"But no more Bitcoin."

"Is Procter and Gamble stock safe enough for you?"

'No. Our government is ever more anti-corporate. I'm not comfortable betting on a U.S. company.:

"Okay, how about $90 in an India ETF and $10 in Bitcoin?"

Sophia sighed. "Okay. Let's turn to a harder issue: communication. When I talk, you only half pay attention and I sense that you want to end the conversation as fast as possible."

"That's only when you complain. We usually don't get anywhere because we've already tried to solve these issues ad nauseam."

"Haven't you ever heard that sometimes, people just want to be heard?"

"How about, each night at dinner, either of us can talk for a few minutes uninterrupted and the other person has to listen carefully."

"Fine. That's something else worth a try. But now, the killer topic: sex. We're down to once a month and I know you're doing it only out of obligation. As far as you're concerned, we'd be celibate"

"We've tried everything. Should we try a sex therapist?"

"Okay, and let's see how well the money and communication experiments work."

They gave each other a perfunctory hug, he went to his laptop, and she phoned a friend.

The sex therapist ended the first session with, "So, shall ve meet ze same time next week?" Albert and Sophia looked at each other knowingly and Sophia bravely said, "We'll get back to you." The therapist sighed.

When they left the office, both broke out in laughter. She imitated the therapist's officious, European accent: "You neet to communikete better unt maybe try a lubrikent or even peacock fezers."

Albert smiled, "Sounds like Dr. Ruth. We would have gotten more benefit from retail therapy. See how I encourage you to spend?"

And they laughed. She said, "See? The therapist brought us together on something!"

The communication and money tactics worked well enough but the lack of sex remained a thorn. They decided not to separate but Albert said, "Should each of us try to have an affair?" This time it was Sophia's turn to sigh and she said, "I guess."

He found Samantha, a marketing manager, to be not smart enough and too sexual.

She found Ethan, a philosophy professor, to be not sexual enough plus, "He smells wrong."

Albert and Sophia agreed to stop that experiment and continue schlepping through life but augmented by the aforementioned money and communication tweaks and by spending more time doing the things they enjoy doing together like watching movies and also, accepting that they'll find the greatest reward in their career.

Albert said, "I think this all is making our marriage better than most." Sophia sighed.

It All Came Down to the Sex

I always had a big sex drive. I was embarrassed when, even after two powerful rounds, I'd often paw at the guy for a third.

Sasin Tipchai, Pixabay, free to reuse

So it was ironic that Jack was the first guy I thought of marrying. Even in the first weeks, he wasn't that eager even for Round 1. My luck, otherwise he was perfect: intelligent, kind, and okay, rich.

Things got, ahem, limp pretty quickly. After just two months, we were down to a perfunctory once a week. We tried everything: communication, fantasies, porn, costumes for God's sake, even a sex therapist. But as we walked out of the session with the shrink, we laughed and agreed that retail therapy would be more therapeutic.

But because Jack was otherwise great and, by that time, my biological clock was ticking pretty loud, we got married. Within months, we were down to near-zero and Jack said, "Please, go have affairs. True love means letting you do what you need to."

To save his feelings, I said I wouldn't do that, but I did do that. First it was just a fling at a conference, then one with a coworker. But then there was Antonio—He was as eager for Round 3 as I was.

When Jack walked in on us, he cried and somehow that made me, right there, tell him that I needed to leave him for Antonio.

A few months later, the infatuation fog with Antonio had lifted for both of us and, as I'm writing to you, I'm thinking of asking Jack if he'd have me back. But no matter how good Jack is, can I accept a life of celibacy or affairs?

Kissy-Poo

I can remember it like it was yesterday. In the bed, Melissa turned to me: "Kissy-Poo?"

"Again?, I smiled.

And she hopped on me for the third time that night.

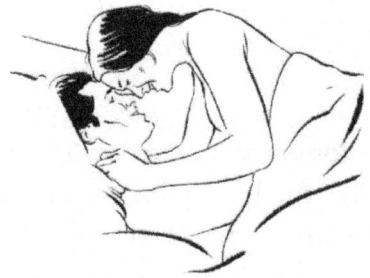

With permission, 18/1 Graphics Studio

I moaned, "I'll love you forever." She whispered, "I want your baby." I laughed, "Three babies!"

Melissa was my first love. I had hoped it could be that way with other women, but the fireworks never exploded. But Melissa was so pretty, so funny, so good in bed!

Two years later

My lawyer argued, "Your honor, when my client was at work, in violation of the divorce decree, she absconded with the armoire."

Her lawyer countered, "Your honor, she was so distraught by her husband having hidden $25,000 that he didn't list in the Disclosure of Assets."

My lawyer tried again: "My client had reason to be distraught. He's being required to pay a ridiculous amount of alimony, excuse me your honor, spousal support. He felt the armoire was tiny compensation."

One year later

Here I am again, giggling in bed, this time with Cindy: Again I'm thinking, "Should I ask her to marry me?"

A Pier

The floor-to-ceiling window overlooked a pier that jutted out into the ocean. It was the perfect backdrop for an inspiring speech and for murder.

With permission, 18/1 Graphics Studio

Kevin, the CEO, intoned like a revival preacher, "It is so exciting to see you here at our 2023 offsite. Our wonderful products are not our most important product. Our most important product? Our employees: You!"

Amanda, a marketing manager, thought, "What a crock."

"Of course, our product line is worthy of you. Just think about how well-priced our bronze line is, how our silver line perfectly balances price and quality, and our platinum product? Best in class!"

She thought, "Yeah, with a lower re-purchase rate than our competitors'."

As Kevin continued stoking the troops, Amanda's mind wandered to the pier. She thought, "Kevin said he couldn't swim. So when he finishes, I'll ask him to watch the sunset with me from the pier."

"And I am so excited that I, no, we are having this offsite. I know it will be awesome." He smiled too broadly and applauded the audience. The audience clapped just enough to stay out of trouble.

After, employees lined up to praise Kevin. When the last suck-up left, Amanda adjusted her blouse so just a bit of cleavage showed, sashayed up, and asked him, "Want to watch the sunset?"

Kevin thought, "She just filed a grievance against me. What's this about?" His wiser self would have declined but he was riding the high of his keynote and the praise, suppressing that both were BS, plus the flirtation, so he agreed.

As they reached the end of the pier, Amanda got cold feet. So she worked herself up by arguing with him. "I still can't believe you wouldn't come with me to the abortion!"

Kevin replied, "There was nothing I could have done to help."

"That's not the point. Haven't you ever heard of the need for support? Guys are clueless."

"Stop playing the gender card. Women's way isn't the only way. Support that accomplishes nothing is stupid."

"Only a guy could say that. Besides, you're the CEO. There's a power imbalance and you took advantage of it."

"You're not my direct report."

"That doesn't negate the power imbalance. And you also showed what a sexist you are when you apologized for not coming to the abortion and I said, 'Put your money where your mouth is: Since you claim to care so much about your employees, create an onsite child care center.' And you said that funding it would be unfair to the childless and to the shareholders. Fuck the shareholders!"

"My position was reasonable and principled. I caved only when you threatened to go public with our affair. I think I'm going to tell the board and the media that you used a sleazy, bargain-basement, unproven contractor and pocketed the difference."

"And I'm going to tell all to the board and the media, including that you dared claim you weren't the father!"

"Oh really? Well, Amanda, long ago, I had a vasectomy. So I couldn't be the father! Want to see? I'll show that to the board and the media. A picture is worth a thousand words."

Of course, Amanda was aware that Kevin might not be the father. She had slept with two other guys at the time. But all that feigned resentment about the affair and abortion accomplished her goal of getting worked up enough to get rid of him and end her worries about him going public with her embezzlement, and now, her false paternity claim.

He started to lower his pants to show his vasectomy, which gave her the chance to shove him into the deep, rough water.

"No! Amanda, you know I can't swim! Please save me!"

It was one thing for Amanda to imagine Kevin drowning, another to see him gasping, dying. So she dove in, helped him to a stanchion, and they climbed up.

They plodded back to the hotel with a lot to think about.

At the closing session, Kevin and Amanda held hands as they strode to center stage. Both applauded the audience. Only a few audience members applauded, tepidly.

Kevin enthused, "I have a special announcement. I've been so impressed with Amanda Frost that I am promoting her to vice-president!"

Romance: Endings

Seven Kisses

I've never been much of a kisser. So I didn't even notice that my parents never kissed me.

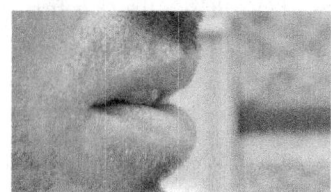

peakpx, CC0

The first kiss I remember was from my doggie, Daisy. It felt good, sweet. I loved my doggie and considering her licking a sign of love, although maybe she just liked my skin's saltiness.

2. My first human kiss was at day camp, maybe age 8. They were showing a movie and a pretty girl—I didn't even know her name—was sitting next to me. I kissed her on the cheek. She didn't slap me. She smiled.

3. That's all there was until my junior year of high school. Laura was, like me, quiet. We liked museums and cafes. On our first date, we did the obligatory peck but I'm not counting that. After two hours at MOMA debating the extent to which minimalist art was aesthetic, political, or giving the finger to convention, we strolled out, and under a tree in Central Park, I felt a stirring, one of kinship as well as sexuality, and I kissed her, for a long time. Not the slurpy, out-of-your-mind kind, the savoring kind.

4. Of course, there was The Kiss at my wedding. I felt I was playing a role, the role of groom, with another character, the minister, ordering, "You may kiss the bride." As soon as I got the order, I kissed her—not too short or it would suggest a bad marriage but not too long or ardent or it would seem like showing off. It was a public display of affection appropriate to having just made a lifetime vow of fidelity in front of our well-wishers.

5. After a year, while we had agreed that no matter what, we'd kiss each other every morning and before we went

to bed, we drifted from that. And the kisses became more sterile, until we stopped.

6. A few years later, as our ardor for each other waned, at a conference, I had a fling. The kiss was electric but even by the end of the conference, the wattage had declined. It became clear to me that affairs weren't the answer. They were sparklers that risked burning your hand and that quickly fizzled.

7. It's now 80 years later and I'm writing to you from my deathbed. I mustered just enough energy to lift my head to reach the cheek of my wife who was leaning down. I'm glad I could kiss her, sad that soon, I never would again.

Not Your Usual 50th Anniversary

After 34 years at a large company, I took the bait of the incentive to retire. Honestly, it wasn't just the money, I was kinda glad to walk away from a couple of my recent screw-ups.

Creazilla, Public Domain

But I was terrified of the statistic—The average man lives only two years after retirement. Sure, many people retire because they're already sick, but there probably also is some truth to retirement itself being deadly—We all need to feel useful, not out to pasture, not irrelevant. That may be especially true for men, for whom work is often central. Quietly, many men find more meaning in work than in family. And there's no question that men live six years shorter than women and spend their last decade in worse health. Yet all we see is another run for breast cancer. But I digress.

My nervousness about retirement was fueled further by the fact I'd be with my wife 24/7/365. But I bit the bullet—a somewhat apt metaphor. While I was still working, my wife had tolerated my occasional rants about media bias and its assault on white men. But now, with me home all the time, she couldn't take it. She'd walk out of the room or even yell, "Enough!"

And *I* couldn't take her noise— the daily and unnecessary vacuuming, the incessant TV, her thumping Zumba videos. A main reason I retired was to get peace and quiet and instead I got noise. I often escaped to the backyard or to a coffee shop but hated having to banish myself from the home I had worked so hard to afford.

But I couldn't escape from my wife using my retirement as a tool to get me to do what she had long pushed for: travel more, see the grandkids more, take dance lessons. "Seymour, you're 74 years old. It's time to cash in that lifetime of work and have fun!" She refused to accept that I found work a wiser use of my time than "fun."

Our 50th anniversary was coming up and I dreaded it— She insisted on throwing a party, a big one. "If we don't celebrate this, what *will* we celebrate?!" I couldn't stop her and then I thought of something. "Stella, I want it to be a 50th-anniversary divorce party. We are better off separate."

I was surprised at her response. Her pride wounded, she didn't want to beg to stay together, to use all the levers I thought she would pull: "Think of the kids, all our history, that we'll want each other in our old age." She just whispered, "Okay."

So she sent out the invitations: "Come celebrate Seymour and Stella's 50th anniversary. We'll be making a surprise announcement."

I planned to put a positive spin on it: "In honor of our 50 years together, we have decided to do something to help ensure that our next 50 are fresh and new—We're divorcing."

But at the moment of truth, right before I said, "We're divorcing," I said, trying to sound sure, "To help ensure that our next 50 are fresh and new, we're…committed to finding the new in each other."

Everyone applauded and I approached the stunned Stella, kissed her, and she relaxed.

A Few Hundred Years in Purgatory with My Wife—No Biggie

I had been the music director at the Church of the Immaculate Heart for 47 years. Some but not all of the choir appreciated my perfectionism. I'd often say, "The loftier the voices, the more you please the Lord."

Lawrence OP, Flickr, CC 2.0

When my health was failing for the final time, the priest visited my bedside and suggested I write my own requiem. I tried to balance solemnity with hope, quietude with energy. I had no idea if my requiem was any good.

On Easter Sunday, I was too ill to come to Mass but when the doorbell rang, I was well enough to wheel myself to the door, barely. And there stood two parishioners, who wheeled me to the church for the Easter service. They wanted to put me in the front but, attempting to be a good Christian, I asked to be toward the back.

As the choir sang my requiem, I cried, and moreso when a little boy in the next row peeked at me and asked his mom, too loudly, "Why does that man have to die?" His mother gave Catholicism's doctrinal explanation: "He'll go to a better place, first to purgatory and once he's been purified, to heaven."

The next week, I got worse and thanks to God's grace, I died in my sleep.

When I next woke up, I was at the Pearly Gates and St. Peter was checking his iPad to see what to do with me. "Good news. No hell for you, just a few hundred years of fiery purification in purgatory. Then, it's up to heaven—barring any new rules from above or from the government.

St. Peter must have seen my look of disappointment. All my life, I had tried to be a good husband, a good music director, a good person, yet I got just the standard treatment? But the loving St. Peter pulled out his wallet and gave me a seven-day pass to heaven after which, yes, I'd need the hundreds of years in purgatory before I got a permanent all-rides pass.

I bowed and thanked St. Peter. Suddenly, the Pearly Gates opened and with a wave of his mighty hand, he motioned me to the up escalator.

Dutiful in heaven as on earth, my first responsibility was to look down on or I should say, down *to*, my wife. I always loved her. Alas, she always viewed me less as the love of her life and more as a necessary neutral.

What she valued most about me was that I was her conscience. So when I saw her reach for a second piece of chocolate cake, I, as angel, floated down and whispered in her ear, "Are you sure?" She stopped.

When a "friend" wanted to invest the money I had left to her in a "sweet deal," I whispered, "No. Vanguard." She listened.

When she started an affair with the parish's bad boy, I whispered, "You deserve better." She listened and instead took up with Bob, the nicest man I knew.

But Bob soon dumped her. She was bereft and couldn't pull herself out of it. But she could pull out a bottle of sleeping pills. I whispered, "No." She opened the bottle and louder I said, "No." She got a glass of water and poured the whole bottle of pills into her hand and, as loudly as this angel could yell, I screamed, No!" But she took them all and died.

Now, I was the bereft one because of my inability to stop her and because my seven-day pass was expiring. I plodded down the escalator. St. Peter shook his head and, with said mighty hand, pointed to an imposing iron door engraved, *Purgatory*. Nervously, I entered to see the purification flames and the sweating masses, including my wife.

I considered trying to return to St. Peter to ask if he thought I'd be happier in hell but decided that a few hundred years with my wife in purgatory would be no biggie.

A Couple in Retirement

Luke trudged out of the drugstore and sighed. "My hearing isn't that bad. I don't want to look old. I don't want to accept that I am old."

And with that out of his system, he trudged back in and bought a hearing aid. After saying hello to his wife, Christine, he escaped to his study to program it.

With permission, 18/1 Graphics Studio

For once, oblivious to the arthritis pain that made getting up difficult, he bounced up to see if he wouldn't so often ask, "What?!"

"So, what's new, Christine?"

"Well, you're not going to like this but our granddaughter is going to a Catholic high school."

He heard that all right: "Religion, ouch. Such bull."

She retorted, "Spoken like the clueless atheist you are."

He turned off his hearing aid and slunk back to his study. "At least she didn't notice I was wearing a hearing aid."

He tried to see if the hearing aid helped him in listening to podcasts on his phone. He tried Lex Fridman, yes! Lunar Society, not so good— the show is poorly mic'd. Then he tried the playlist that his son set up for him on his phone—Awesome!

Christine called in, "I also booked us on a cruise. We're boring each other. We need to shake things up."

He didn't hear what she said so he turned his hearing aid back on and padded in.

"What did you say?"

"I said, "I booked us on a cruise, on the Royal Empress."

"I hate cruises: floating apartment buildings with rooms so small they wouldn't put welfare recipients in them. And they're monuments to gluttony. Plus, they charge lowball prices to get you onboard and then charge extra for everything except breathing."

"Luke, do try to have a good time."

"What I'll probably do is gain weight and maybe end up in the ship hospital, maybe even be one of the people who, on every cruise, drops dead from overeating, or

Relationship Stories

gets COVID. And you know I can't resist all that "free" food. I can't believe you booked us on a cruise."

He kept complaining. For example, when they pulled into the dock's parking lot, "Loan sharks wouldn't change that much." and "I can't believe how long the line is just to get on the damn boat."

"It's not a boat. It's a ship. By the way, I've chosen the sitdown-dinner option rather than the buffet. You'll eat less— See? I care about you."

"You chose it because you don't want to spend so much time with me. They'll seat us with other people, probably the shallow types that tend to go on cruises."

I didn't book any of the excursions. I wanted your input.

Those are ripoffs.

Stop!

All right, pick an excursion, any excursion.

How about the bus tour? It's the least expensive.

I might not want to get back on the bus with you.

Not a bad idea.

They disembarked at Heaven Bay, the cruise line's private island.

In the manufactured-for-tourists chachka huts, Luke and Christine separated a bit when she wanted to look at sarongs— and he took it as a chance to escape.

She called and called him to no avail, searched the area, but didn't look in the one place she was sure he wouldn't be in: the church. After all, he even cringed at Christmas carols. But there he was in the belfry, enjoying Christine's franticness. "For once, she cares where I am. Of course, that's only because she doesn't want to get stranded."

Christine told the bus driver who waited as long as possible but finally, after talking with the ship's captain. he said, "Lady, the ship ain't gonna wait any longer. We're going. You can come if you like." She did.

After just a few hours, Luke was bored with painted coconuts, straw hats, and steel-drum music. So he boarded another ship at the dock.

Their staff, of course, checked his documents and then called the Royal Empress to be sure Luke wasn't a terrorist, and let him on.

Back home, Luke and Christine were more separate than ever, his hearing aid turned off more and more. So he didn't hear when she said, "I've just booked an around-the-world-in-80- days cruise. I'm going by myself."

Birth and Death

Yes, I had told Victoria that I wanted children. And at the time, I did. I was infatuated with her, with the idea of having and raising a child, and maybe having someone to care for us in our old age.

With permission, 18/1 Graphics Studio

The desire to have kids was fueled by our friends who had them. They emphasized the positives, if only to not seem cold or like bad parents. And of course, our grandparents were salivating for grandkids.

But then, worries intruded: "Bye-bye freedom. Waking up in the middle of the night. Fighting with the kid about homework. Will I be even a good parent? My job isn't that secure. Can we afford to have a baby? And what if our baby isn't normal?"

I decided to not say any of that to Vicki. I could just imagine her reaction: "What?! You said you wanted a baby! So what do you want me to do now? Get an abortion? No!" I could picture her screaming, then crying, then miserable through her pregnancy, and blaming me forever for spoiling her motherhood.

My worry about an abnormal baby was justified. Lou Jr. was born with an Apgar score of 6, which predicts low IQ.

The first time Vicki and I had sex after Lou was born, my erection wasn't as hard as usual. And over the next months, I became softer and softer until I couldn't have intercourse. In frustration, Victoria said, "You're doing this to punish me!"

Of course, that wasn't true and I got so angry that I did something I thought I'd never do: I slapped her in the face, hard. Even in retrospect, I sort of feel she deserved it but I do recognize that hitting a woman is strictly verboten.

In the next months, we didn't even try to have sex and our relationship declined further, in part because we didn't have sex available to balm life's problems. And atop regular problems, there was Lou, who was difficult, low IQ or not.

He was what Victoria called "fussy," which I thought was an understatement.

And yes, once at 3 AM, when Lou was already six months old and was up yelling half the night, and when I finally got back to bed exhausted after unsuccessfully trying to calm him, I actually said it: "You know, Vicki, Lou is a nightmare!" Victoria seethed, "That hurts me more than even that slap. Much more."

A month later, Vicki expanded on a Lorena Bobbitt: On the night before the trash would get picked up, she poisoned my dinner and then, with the help of my chain saw, cut me up, threw me into a big black garbage bag and into the trash bin for the next morning's pickup.

She got away with it. She simply told the cops that I had gone for a walk and never returned. The investigation turned up nothing, so the cops assumed it was just another case of a spouse walking out, and they tossed the case into the cold-case file.

I'm writing to you from purgatory hoping that Vicki feels at least ambivalent about what she did.

"I Wanted My Husband to Die"

I always flirted a lot but was married, so I didn't cheat. Well, I did once, but it was no big deal.

The problem was our marriage. You see, I'm a normal, fun-loving person. I love travel, dancing, doing things with family. My husband liked none of that. Mainly he just liked to work.

The Advocacy Project, Flickr, CC 2.0

And when we conversed and I would talk about normal topics—friends, family, pop culture, spirituality, clothes, decorating, cooking, gardening, even current events—he just wanted to escape to his bedroom... to work.

He was like his father. He didn't work for the money. He'd do it for free. He'd *pay* to work. Work was just what he cared about. He actually said, "The meaning of life lies in productivity." And I knew he'd never change.

Of course, I thought about divorcing him but that would have been too painful, especially given who he was: He would have been very hurt and he was very smart. Even if we had started out agreeing to have an amicable do-it-yourself divorce, it would have devolved into a war, with him hiring a killer lawyer and giving him all the ammunition he needs. In defense, I'd hire my killer lawyer and years later, we'd both have been pounded and poorer.

When I was 72, my bad back started to be a real problem. It became hard to bend over and to get in and out of the car. I walked like an old lady. It was a reminder that life's clock was ticking.

About a year ago, my husband asked me, "Do you wish I were dead?" Of course, I said no but it got me thinking.

Not long afterward, he had a stroke and said, "I hope I die. I don't want you to have to care for a vegetable." He did become kind of a vegetable. The main reason I didn't put him in a home was that I was afraid my friends would think I was cruel. Maybe I am.

Last week, he died, and today the people who came to the house after the funeral just left. I was good: I put on a sad face, I reminisced, I told them I was grieving. But if I'm honest with you, my main thought is, "How soon can I start to live, even to flirt?"

At Work

A Loyal Gardener

Genevieve had been Stanley's gardener for 43 years. Now 73, despite her bad back, she continued. Yes, she needed the money but she had seen the other people in Stanley's life come and go, and even steal—A housecleaner had giggled, "I steal one piece of silverware at a time. I'm now at a service for 4. He never noticed!"

Maasaak, Wikimedia, CC 4.0

One day, Genevieve's back was bothering her more than usual, but Stanley was excited about the new rose bush he bought and in his quiet way let her know that he was eager to see it planted. He even showed her the spot.

She dug and dug, her back hurting more and more. She knew that roses like a deep hole and had dug almost down to the ideal 18 inches when her shovel hit something that sounded like wood —maybe a branch that hadn't fully decomposed? She struggled down to her knees to push away the soil that was still covering it—It was a box, an antique wooden box. She slowly opened it, and inside was note on ivory vellum paper. It was written in turquoise ink in a relaxed handwriting:

Dear Genevieve,

I knew your back was hurting particularly badly today and so, before I made my final decision, I decided to put you to one more test—You've already passed 43 years of working for me, *loyally, responsibly. That's an incredible test. But you have just dug a tough, tough hole despite your bad back just because I hinted that I wanted you to. I have worked hard all my life and spent little, so I've accumulated a fair amount. I'm old now and want to see the benefit of my work and savings so, rather than put you in my will, I have transferred most of my life's savings, $250,000, into your checking account. That is my way, Genevieve, of showing you that I love you.*

Of course, Genevieve cried, ran into the house, and hugged Stanley.

I wish that were the end of the story but it isn't.

When Genevieve told her friends and family about it, they all urged her to retire from gardening, especially with her bad back. But she explained that she wanted to be loyal to Stanley until she absolutely couldn't do the gardening anymore.

So Genevieve continued, and although her back slowly kept degenerating, she was still able to do her work. But at age 78, something snapped. She could no longer even stand without seven-level pain. Her doctor and the second-opinion doctor said that her only option was surgery although it was far from sure that the benefits would outweigh the risks. And Medicare agreed. Its denial of coverage read, "At age 78, the risk-reward ratio of the surgery is insufficient to provide coverage."

Genevieve felt it was surgery or suicide so she paid for it out of the money Stanley had given her. Alas, she required a revision surgery, which wiped out all her money.

But finally, Genevieve was pretty much out of pain and could walk. Stanley invited her to live with him forever, to enjoy retirement together, and she gratefully accepted.

"The Bitch"

In a car assembly plant, I'm the foreman, forewoman, whatever you want to call me. Either way, they call me, The Bitch.

Before I got promoted to foreman, they'd straggle in late. But I told them that from then on, more than one minute late, they'll be docked. Too many excuses are BS and I can't tell which are. They figured that because I'm a woman, I'd fall for child-care excuses. Nope: Doctor's note or it's dock time.

Carol Highsmth, Picryl, CC

And when I caught a guy throwing a bolt into a differential and laughing to the guy next to him on the assembly line, "Let's see if QA can figure out *that* rattle," I fired him on the spot. Yeah, the union filed a grievance but I wouldn't back down and I won, I fucking won.

As you might guess, I'm glad to get home each day. It's hard being The Bitch. The guys probably think that when I get home, I beat up puppy dogs. But truth is, I usually put on new-age relaxing music, cut flowers from my condo's patio, arrange them nicely, get a glass of wine, and read romance novels.

Let me tell you why the Jekyll and Hyde routine.

When I was on the assembly line and even when I was a student, I saw too many people view nicey-nicey as a sign of weakness. They know they can get away with shit. They respond only to boundaries and consequences.

But why do I care so much that I'm willing to be called The Bitch and come home every day exhausted? Because every customer who gets a car that doesn't work right is a human being that I've made sad or angry. Every investor in our company, who entrusted us with his or her hard-earned money hoping to save for a car, home, college, or retirement, will lose money if our cars suck—They'll buy a Toyota.

I'm proud to be The Bitch and if and when I ever have kids, I'll teach them to be a bitch.

"It's Not My Job to Make You Coffee"

"Martelle, I'm swamped. Would you make me coffee?"

TrentSD, Flickr, CC2.0

Trying not to sound angry, Martelle said, "Michael, you know it's not my job to make you coffee. I'm your administrative assistant. That means Word docs, scheduling, and screening your email. It doesn't make me your maid."

"Never mind." Michael tried to say it evenly but it came out angry. He thought, "You're marginal, Martelle. I'd fire you except that it would be so difficult."

It's understandable that Martelle refused. After all, her mother *was* a maid and proud that Martelle had gotten Microsoft-certified in Word, PowerPoint, and even Excel. Plus, the media had endlessly told Martelle that BIPOCs are marginalized. In her mother's words, "When you face injustice, you must stand up if not rise up."

Yet it's also understandable that Michael would have liked to fire Martelle. Especially when HR and other bosses stress collaboration, it doesn't seem like much, when he's busy, to ask his admin to make him a cup of coffee. Indeed Michael, despite his masters in computer science from CalTech, sometimes has to do busywork that a high school dropout could do. And Michael's views had roots deeper than colleges and media. His father was an engineer who believed in, "Unless you're sick, no excuses. Just get it done."

But Martelle had had enough. This wasn't the first time Michael "asked" her to make coffee. Worse, when she made a mistake, he'd often sigh condescendingly. And although she hadn't had a pay increase in 18 months, he turned her down, indeed hinted that she might have to accept a pay cut. She documented all that and filed a grievance with her union, which in turn, sent it to HR and to the EEOC, demanding a hearing.

When Michael saw the complaint, he quit and became a self-employed app developer. He's working on a better approach to matching job seekers with employers.

Fired

Damn the younger generation—no respect for tradition, let alone for the wealthy, most of whom have worked long and hard and gotten rich because they provided enough value that many other people were willing to give their hard-earned money.

Jared Tarbell, Flickr, CC 2.0

So I opened La Grande Pizza, which for $100 a pie, gives you the pizza experience of a lifetime. All the toppings are the finest in the world. For example, they say, "You don't want to know how sausage or laws are made." Well, I want to you to see how my sausage is made. No cow eyes here—Filet mignon with just the right spices. And instead of the cardboardy crust you get elsewhere, mine is filled with flavor and slightly crispy on the outside and chewy when you bite in. The secret is my 1,000-degree pizza oven that I brought over personally from Palermo.

Yet my waiters act as though they're working at Pizza Hut. I train them and train them but they so often forget or spite me. Spite. Yes, that's what I mainly think, spite!

I used to treat them so well—pay them well, train them well, praise them, forgive them. But it didn't work well.

Relationship Stories

So I decided I needed to be the boss like in the old country. They hated me but it worked.

Every time I caught them, I'd scare them. For example, I had trained them to keep one hand behind their back as they served the pizza, while gently lowering it onto the table. If I caught a waiter acting like it was Pizza Hut and slamming down a pie, I'd tell the waiter, "I need to see you." He'd come terrified to the kitchen, I'd get in his face, bore into his eyes, seethe, "One more time and you're fired!" and stride out to be nice to the customers.

That didn't work well enough but they were too scared to quit. After all, I paid them much more than other restaurants did. But many of them still sucked. So then I decided to hit them where it hurts, what they care about: money. I started docking them $10 every time I caught them, even something as small as not ending a wine-pour with a gentle circling and lifting of the bottle, an elegant flourish. They hated me even more for docking them.

Then, one night, after the last customer was gone, the waiter who I thought I could most trust said he had a surprise for me in the kitchen. I thought, "Well, finally, some appreciation. After all, my birthday was coming up." I was wrong.

When I got there, all the waiters, bussers, and chefs circled around me and tied me to a chair. My trusted waiter said, "You always threaten to fire us. Well, now we're going to fire you! He opened the door to the 1,000-degree oven and said, "Now Pizza Man, you're going to be a House Special." They lifted me up as I screamed, "I'm sorry, I'm sorry" and they stopped.

Family

Spoon

After I finished high school, everyone thought I'd go to Poland's most prestigious college, the University of Warsaw, but my father's fabric business was struggling to stay alive. The Nazi invasion was making even Christians nervous about spending on discretionary items.

Suzi Jones, Picryl, Public Domain

The town we lived in was safe—No one locked their door. So one day—and yes it was 1942, so we shouldn't have been so surprised—there was an unusually loud knock on the door. It was two Nazis in black boots. Unlike in the movies, they didn't yell. One was silent and the other whispered, "You will be out of your house with only what you can carry by noon tomorrow, or else."

The next day at noon, four Nazis came to the door again and yelled, "Rouse!" And they dragged my mom, dad, sister, and me onto a truck.

They took us to a place in the forest called Ponary. One Nazi grabbed my sister and dragged her away to a barrack. The other Nazis threw the rest of us into a pit, whereupon they shot most of us to death, including my

Relationship Stories

mother and father. They left a few of us for a reason I was soon to learn.

I had rarely cried before but then I sobbed, hard. Then they threw gasoline onto the dead people and used a flame thrower to set them on fire. I threw up. Then they threw shovels and lime into the pit and yelled, "Now, you bury them or you'll go too. You bury them nice and you'll get food."

That night, we took our spoons, dug a hole under the barbed wire, and escaped. At least we tried. The Nazis shot all of us except me. I had managed to run deeper into the forest.

For days, I survived only by eating nuts and berries from the trees. Then I saw a cabin in the distance. I was exhausted but seeing it, I practically ran there.

An old woman answered the door and on seeing me, unshaven, dirty, smelling of something that had burned, she must have been scared. "What do you want?!"

I explained that I'm harmless. Still she said, "Go away." I had to think of something. I saw her wearing a big cross and there was a picture of Jesus on her wall, so I said, "I'm a priest who the Nazis chased away. Can I bless you?"

She softened and I tried to make up some Catholic-sounding blessing, and she then took care of me for three years until the Americans liberated the Jews.

I was put on a train to England and then on a cargo boat to Ellis Island, New York City. I didn't have a penny, no education, no family, no English, only the scars of the Holocaust.

The only job I could get was shining shoes. I didn't want to do that forever so I went to night school to learn English. My teacher said I learned quickly and that I should go to college. So I went to Bronx Community College and then City College of New York, and then, Albert Einstein Medical School.

That was 50 years ago.

Today, I was looking at the patients I was to see today and saw my sister's name! I assume she survived Ponary because the Nazis thought she was sexy.

Now, both of us were far from sexy. I am a year from retirement and she looked even older than I do. And when I saw her chart, I saw why: She was referred to me, a cardiologist, because her primary care doctor diagnosed her with end-stage heart failure.

I couldn't wait for her appointment but was dreading having to confirm the diagnosis. I'll just say that we hugged for 20 minutes.

This story is derived from my father's true story. He was one of the men to escape from the Ponary death camp where, indeed, he had been forced to bury the Jews that the Nazis shot. They did try to escape by digging a tunnel with their spoons. It's also true that after the war, my father was dumped on a cargo boat and dropped in the Bronx, where the only job he could get was as a factory worker. He went to night school to learn English and, while he didn't become a doctor, he made a middle-class living owning a small store in a tough neighborhood in Brooklyn. My dad, Boris Nemko, is my greatest inspiration.

Story Time

My son never outgrew his love of my reading to him. Nor did I.

Robert Couse—Baker, Flickr, CC2.0

It started ordinarily enough. From when Jerry was a baby, I read to him: First, Hop on Pop, Cat in the Hat, The Little Engine That Could, you know, the usual hits. We particularly loved The Carrot Seed. In that story, a little boy planted a carrot seed and everyone in his family said it wouldn't grow, but the boy kept watering it and watering it, and finally it came up "just as the little boy always knew it would." My son mainly loved that the boy turned out to be right. I tried, not altogether successfully, to explain that the story was about the wisdom of being persistent when you're confident you're correct.

Then, when Jerry was 8, we read The Giving Tree and talked about what the story meant. My son thought it was, "Save the trees." My son was unusually mature, so I felt I could try a more mature explanation: The story is about life sometimes becoming less and less happy. It also asks, "What is too much sacrifice?" and "When you give a person a finger, does it make them want an arm?" As usual, we ended with a hug and a promise that we would have story time forever.

When Jerry was around 10, our favorite was James and the Giant Peach— a welcome break from reality:

> *But the peach ... ah, yes ... the peach was a soft, stealthy traveler, making no noise as it floated along. And several times during that long silent night ride high up over the middle of the ocean in the moonlight, James and his friends saw things that no one had ever seen before.*

When Jerry was 16, our favorite was The Lottery and we discussed how groupthink can make regular people do or at least ignore horrific things, for example, citizens of Nazi Germany, the snitches of Stalinist USSR, and some warrior-lemmings today.

When Jerry was 20 and away at college, I'd read aloud over the phone. I particularly remember The Secret Life of Walter Mitty. Walter escapes into fantasy to avoid being suppressed by his strong wife. Surprisingly, that triggered quite an argument. Jerry insisted on the importance of following your dreams while I made the case for being realistic, which made him insist he was going to take big risks. That got me scared and a little angry. But we got off the phone saying— and meaning it— that we'll always love each other.

I'll fast-forward. As I'm writing this, I'm on my deathbed, Jerry just read The Giving Tree again to me and said, "Your interpretation 70 years ago was right The book is about life's path from exuberance to disillusionment, fatigue, and death. And I promise to read to my kids forever."

Not a bad capstone to a lifetime of story time.

Empty

My stroller was more basic than most of the others'. Still, I liked sitting in the park where the moms hung out.

Bicanski, pixnio, CC0

But I always stayed on a bench in the corner to avoid any questions. Nevertheless, one of them finally came up to me and asked to see my baby—You see, I always kept the canopy down. I told her, "Maybe some other time." Puzzled and feeling awkward, she murmured, "Okay," walked back to the others, and started whispering to them. They began leaned forward and whispering to each other.

Then, one of them strolled over to me and "accidentally" lifted my stroller's canopy. She said, "Oops, sorry" but peered in and saw the blanket, which had the bulge underneath.

She said, "Aren't you afraid your baby won't get enough air?" I said no and, without asking, she pulled back the blanket and saw the doll.

I lied: "I had a miscarriage and that's one way I'm grieving." She said, "I understand." My body language told her that I wanted to be alone again, she got the message, and plodded away.

Of course, that made me think about the truth that I try hard to suppress. I had been in my ninth month and terrified of having a bowling ball come out of me and even more terrified of having to raise it for 18 years—the stress, the cost, the loss of freedom. So I searched and searched to find a doctor who'd perform a late-term abortion. They all said no, that doing it in the ninth month isn't an abortion, it's infanticide. All of them said no, except one.

Yes, I feel guilty. Yes, I can see the baby in my mind's eye and that's painful. But I still think it was the right thing to do.

I got up from my bench and joined the group.

Lip Gloss

Julie and her mom, Natalie, were headed toward the Revlon display when Julie stopped at the Bonne Bell lipstick rack.

"You're too young," Natalie said.

"Other girls wear it!"

With permission, 18/1 Graphics Studio

"I don't care about other girls. You're 11. You don't want to look like a tramp."

"What's a tramp?"

"Never mind." She pulled Julie away and to the Revlon display, where Natalie scrutinized the lipsticks with the focus of a diamond buyer: On the Mauve, Blushing Nude ...

Julie got angrier seeing her mother bask in that rainbow of adornment. While Natalie was trying on Bare Affair, Julie tiptoed back to Bonne Bell, stuffed a Minnie Mouse lip gloss into her pocket, and returned to her mom, who was now on lipstick five: Nude Fury.

Natalie asked, "How do I look?" Julie muttered, "Just great, mom."

They paid, a man followed them out, and stopped them: "Young lady, I need to see what's in your pocket."

Natalie said, "I didn't take anything. Here's my receipt."

"Not you, lady, the kid."

Natalie protested, "Julie didn't do anything."

"Yeah, kid, show your mom what nothing you did." Shaking, Julie looked up at the man, hoping for a reprieve but he was stony, so she pulled the lip gloss from her pocket.

He said, "You're lucky we don't prosecute under $25, but Mom, you better deal with her." And he strode away.

Julie got a surprise. Her mom hugged her and said, "When I was your age, I did the same thing. Well, not exactly— it was a different color."

Wonder Woman

I hate that I had reached the mandatory retirement age for National Park police: 57. I still feel young, love my job, my coworkers, the park visitors, and most of all, that my "office" was Yellowstone National Park.

Yeah, I have a pension, but now I spend too much time pacing: pacing my house, pacing my backyard, pacing the park.

With permission, 18/1 Graphics Studio

So I was glad to be invited to my granddaughter Chloe's 2nd birthday party. What gift to buy? My daughter said that Chloe likes music, so I found a toy piano for toddlers on Amazon: just eight keys but it can make the sound of an electric piano, an organ, even a DJ scratcher.

But after Chloe tore open the gift wrapping, she pouted, "I wanted Wonder Woman." When I asked whether she wanted to try the piano, she shook her head. To try to entice her, I plunked out the only song I knew, Mary Had a Little Lamb, but she turned away. Grandparents spoil so I said, "Okay, I'll get you Wonder Woman, Chloe," and bought the cheapest one I could find.

I kept the toy piano because it was a hassle to ship it back to Amazon. I'd occasionally, trial-and-error, plunk out other simple songs like Old McDonald and Row, Row, Row Your Boat. Then I wrote words to them about what I know: parks, cops, even an anti-drug PSA, and posted them on YouTube.

When I next visited Chloe, I brought the little piano and played my ditties for her, yes, in part to show her what she missed. She said, "I want it!"

I asked, "Where's Wonder Woman?" She replied, "I don't know."

Playing Hooky

I was so in the mood for waffles. My mom said no because there wasn't time, but I begged and she poured batter into the waffle maker, and I was happy.

Then her phone rang— It was her boss and she forgot about the waffle. When I smelled it burning,

Touch Of Light, Wikimedia, CC4.0

I pulled at her suit and said, "Mommy, mommy, it's burning." She turned off the waffle maker and finished her phone call. When she opened the cover, it was burned. She said a bad word and then, "Take a yogurt from the refrigerator— You'll eat it in the car."

Then I remembered that she had to sign the permission slip for my class field trip to the African-American Civil War Museum. I had a hard time finding it in my backpack and I saw her tapping her foot. She scribbled her signature, grabbed her briefcase, and we rushed to the car.

She didn't even buckle me into the child seat, and she drove fast— She had to slam on her brakes because a light was turning red. When we got to my school, the schoolyard was empty— the kids had already gone in. We raced to the student door but it was locked. My mom said another bad word and we rushed toward the front entrance where we'd have to tell the school secretary why we were late. But before we got to the door, my mom stopped and said, "Let's play hooky!" She called her boss and said that I just got sick and so she didn't have time to get a babysitter. I didn't know that parents lie.

Then she told me that she knows someone who works at a bakery, so we went and saw how croissants are made. You have to put a ton of butter into the dough and then roll it out three times, cut it up, and stack the layers, and somehow that gets you hundreds of layers. Wow!

I was loving watching and especially tasting. Croissants are delicious, especially the chocolate one! It hit me that while I was eating a croissant my class was probably doing math. We are working on something called associative and distributive I don't remember what the other word is.

When we got back in the car, my mother drove us around the cool five-sided building where she works— It's called the Pentagon— It's CIA headquarters. I asked if she's a spy. She laughed and said that she is one of the many people who work there who just read and write things. That was boring so I asked her lots of questions about what it's like to be a spy. Most times she said, "I don't know" or "That's classified. I can't tell you, even though you're my son." But she did tell me that the CIA tried using cats as spies. The cats were equipped with a tiny antenna so they could transmit secret conversations back to the CIA. I was loving hearing about that and imagined that if I were in class now, we'd probably be on spelling or if we were lucky, art— We were learning how to make origami.

My mom drove me back to school. I was in time for social studies. The teacher was talking about the Civil War but I was still thinking about cat spies. I think she saw me daydreaming, so she called on me: "Justin, what was the Civil War about?" I could only come up with, "Freeing the Blacks?" She sighed and said, "Pay attention!" I thought, my day with mom was more important or at least better. I'll ask mom if we can play hooky again tomorrow.

Who to Save?

I have ten-year-old twins. Because they're fraternal, they're different. While similar in intelligence, Matthew is bookish and kind, while Paul is aggressive, often mean.

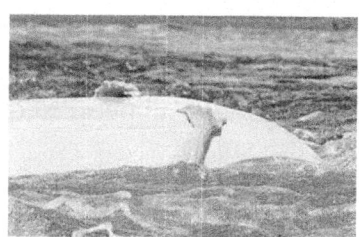
Abkfenris, Flickr, CC 2.0

We often go whitewater kayaking. This day, as usual, they roughhoused, with Paul, of course, the aggressor and Matthew doing his best to tamp things down. Today, that was unsuccessful and they tussled so much that our kayak tipped over, we all fell out and at the worst possible spot: The river was wide and fast.

We were buffeted and buffeted and the further we went, the more separated we were —I was ten yards from either child.

Which child should I try to swim to first? To be honest, in that split second, I instinctively leaned to toward the gentle Matthew, and that is where I headed, whereupon Paul screamed, "What about me?!!!"

I got to Matthew and our only choice was to keep going down the rapids, feet first. Fortunately, we soon were able to grab a tree branch as we watched Paul flail further downriver.

We managed our way onto the riverbank, ran downriver, and just ahead, saw Paul clinging to a rock that jutted up from the rapids. I dove in and brought Paul to shore to join Matthew. We are all fine.

But now, if people were to tell me that they love their children equally or even, as some spiritual people say, that they love all people equally, I'd quietly scoff.

Mother of the Bride

From the first minute, Janet didn't like Dennis. She saw her daughter Emma fall prey to his bad-boy looks and demeanor, something Janet herself had done and swears never again. So it particularly hurt Janet to see Emma be the same fool.

With permission, 18/1 Graphics Studio

Janet tried everything. After Emma and Dennis' first date, Emma came home and asked if she liked Dennis. Janet wanted to yell, "Are you crazy?!" but deliberately pursed her lips and evenly said, "How do you like him?"

Janet prayed that one of them would break it off but they got closer. Janet realized that discouraging them risked Emma doing the opposite. It could even damage the mother-daughter relationship.

Then, Emma came home flashing an engagement ring, whereupon Janet figured she had little to lose. She said, "Even when I went out to dinner with the two of you, I saw his roving eye. And he epitomizes the sleazy salesman; he even bragged about how he manipulates customers to buy. And he doesn't seem to care much about you. To be honest, I think the main thing he likes is your body." Not surprisingly, Emma stormed out.

A few minutes before the ceremony, Janet followed the tradition of joining Emma in her bridal boudoir. Janet realized it was too late to say anything about Dennis, so she just praised Emma's appearance: "I just love your hair and the tiara is the perfect finishing touch ...That dress looks amazing on you."

When the minister intoned, "until death do you part," Janet forced herself to maintain her manufactured smile.

Then the minister asked, "If anyone believes why Dennis and Emma should not be joined in holy matrimony, let them speak now or forever hold their peace."

Janet thought of all the movies she had seen in which someone stopped the wedding. She thought, "Doing that would be the best wedding gift I could give Emma." But Janet just pursed her lips though quickly realized that even that would look bad, so she pasted the smile back on until she was back in her car.

My Daughter is Getting Married

My daughter said, "Dad, I'm getting married."

Raw Pixel, CC0

In the second before I had to respond, I thought about my two failed marriages and other relationships. To buy a bit of time, I said, not effusively, not flatly, "Congratulations."

She probably thought, "That's all, and so tepid? What an asshole." but said only, "Thanks, Dad."

I thought, "She hadn't even told me she was seeing someone. I've been a good father. Why wouldn't she tell me?" But I said only, "Want to tell me about him?"

Relationship Stories

She said, "Her." and probably thought, "What a dinosaur. That's why I don't tell him shit. And I'm sure not going to tell him that she's the one because of the sex." But what she said was, "Well, she's pretty, makes me laugh, and makes more money than I do."

I thought, "You keep insisting you're an independent woman, yet now your fiancée's money is a top reason you're marrying her?" But I said only, "When's the wedding?"

She probably thought, "That's all you need to know about her? Jesus!" But she said only, "June 17, Key West, Smothers Beach."

I thought, "At least it's not some expensive resort but I'm guessing she's still going to hit me up to pay for it." But I said only, "In June, isn't Florida a bit hot?"

She probably thought, "Controlling and negative as usual. Asshole!" But she said, "On the beach it will okay for the ceremony and the reception will be at the La Capitana Resort."

I thought, "Resort. Expensive. Damn it!" but said only, "I see."

She probably thought, "Fucking passive-aggressive" but said, "Dad, Kat's parents don't have much money, they're artists, so I need you to pay for the wedding."

I was furious and couldn't control my face turning apoplectic nor stay with the controlled responses, so I blurted, "You should have consulted me about all this before asking me to pay for it."

She probably thought, "I knew it. Cheap bastard!" Like me, unable to remain controlled, she seethed, "Never mind. I don't want your money. You know, I don't want you at the wedding!" And she stormed out.

June arrived and both of us were too stubborn to give an inch, but on the wedding day, I flew down to Key West and showed up at Smothers Beach a half hour before the ceremony. I merely nodded at her, she nodded back, and whispered to her aunt, who had agreed to walk her down the aisle.

I walked her down the aisle, smiling but fuming.

An MD and His Starving-Artist Child

Yes, I'm tired, often overwhelmed. You'd think after all those years of pre-med, medical school, internship, residency, and setting up a practice, I'd be entitled to a pretty good life.

Raffael Herrmann, CC0.photo, Public Domain

Yet the Medicare and insurance reimbursements keep getting cut. They think doctors are fat cats to be redistributed from, but when you consider the cost of medical school, malpractice insurance, setting up an office and paying staff, I wonder if garbage collectors net more.

And all the idealism that fueled my willingness to endure all of that has faded. Too many non-compliant, non-paying, or know-it-all patients. Too much paperwork only to often get my request for reimbursement denied or cut. And the stress: I'm making life-and-death decisions all the time and sometimes must give bad news, even fatal news. Plus, it's hard to keep up with what's new. My medical journals are piling up unread—It reminds me of why I canceled my subscription to the New Yorker—I kept feeling guilty that I didn't have time to read them.

Yet when my daughter insisted that she didn't want to be a doctor, not even to go to college, but only to art school, I was sad. Art school—that four-year summer camp that too often leads to the cliche, "starving artist," never making enough even to pay back student loans let alone make a living, even a subsistence living. That's especially so in an era of ever-better AI-created art.

So I decided to tell her that I wouldn't pay for art school but would pay for college as long as her major was even vaguely practical. She enrolled at a local state university, which made sense to me. Despite my moderate net income, I'd still get little financial aid and most of what I did get would be a loan that would have to be paid back with interest. And today, the sticker price of four years at a brand-name coastal private college is $300,000+, and not much less at a brand-name out-of-state public college. And that assumes she graduates in four years. It often takes five or longer, and almost half drop out.

When she was home for Christmas, she left her transcript on the kitchen table. It was emblazoned with her major: studio art!

I told her that unless she switched majors, I wouldn't pay. She showed that she is the strong-minded, independent woman I encouraged her to be—She dropped out of college and rather than come back home, she lived with three roommates in a dangerous part of the city. She paid for it with a part-time job as a clerk in an art supply store plus government welfare programs: food stamps, housing subsidy, transportation vouchers, some cash aid, even free admission to tourist attractions like museums.

I came to visit her and found her happy, candidly, happier than I am. She said, "I'd rather be a starving artist than an exhausted, burned-out doctor. Dad, are you sure you shouldn't consider a career change?"

I said no but as I was driving home, I started thinking.

A Gen Z Son Fights His Millennial Dad

The son came home from work at 5:30 to see his dad still at his home-office desk. The son said, "Dude, workday's over. Come on, let's chill."

Rene Rasmussen, Pexels, CC0

His father replied, "Sorry. I'm on a roll and want to get to a good stopping place. It should take me about an hour. Have your joint and, if you want, dinner without me."

"Whatever."

An hour later, Dad was still at it.

The son scoffed, "Really?"

His dad replied, "I care to do a good job."

"Does it really matter whether the company has a 1.5 megaflop to replace its 1.4? All that mainly does is give the salespeople an excuse to pressure customers into upgrading."

"Look, the company has been good to me. I want to do it."

"The company has been good to you? They're only 'good to you' as long as you make them more money than they could get out of a 25-year-old in India. When that stops, you're part of a 'reorg.'"

"And look at you! You look for every excuse to do as little as you can get away with, to 'quiet quit.' You'd rather smoke weed."

"I value work-life balance."

"You have a shallow definition of the meaningful life. Whether or not a company treats me well, I want to do a good job because that, and not funstering, is core to the life well-led.

"You're a fool."

"And you are out of here. I let you come back home figuring I could help you launch your career. But I've clearly failed, plus my largesse seems to have been rewarded by disrespect. Go sink or swim."

"Great idea. I'll pack now."

Father's Day

It was 4:00 and I had almost forgotten it was Father's Day when I passed a hardware store. In the window, a sign said, "Give Dad what he wants: tools."

With permission, 18/1 Graphics Studio

I hadn't gotten what I wanted: a call.

I went to a cafe and thought: Was I a good father? Well, I'm a researcher for political campaigns, not a bad role model. On the other hand, I just couldn't make myself be as involved a parent as my wife had been.

But, yes, really, I deserve to be treated better. He resented my making him even take out the garbage. And yeah, I yelled when his main goal was getting high, but still.

Should I call him? I know he doesn't want me to. After all these years, the mature me would just shrug, but this year somehow I can't. I called, he answered, and hung up on me.

Hide

I've always been reluctant to show my feelings. For example, I tried to remain expressionless when the kids were choosing sides for softball and I got picked later than I thought I deserved to be.

Photo credit: Dries Buytaert, CC4.0

But what my sister did to me made me swear I'd never show my feelings again. One night, when the dog in the movie we were watching died, I cried, a lot. When she asked me why, I explained that it wasn't just that the dog died, it's that I'm scared, no, terrified, of dying.

My sister is two years older than me and so she soon became sophisticated enough to push my buttons. She'd say things like, "After you die, you can never come back. Never. You'll just get eaten by worms." and, "Most people don't die peacefully. They die screaming."

I tried to suppress those thoughts but she wouldn't let me. She taunted me all the time, enjoying seeing me get teary. Worse, she made sure the fear remained top-of-mind. For example, one evening, I came into my bedroom to find that, into my bed's wooden headboard. she had etched the words "worms" and "screaming!"

So as I grew up, I made sure to, for example, never show a woman how much I cared for her. I was afraid she'd use my caring to extract what she wanted from me—

expensive gifts, fancy vacations, and so on. So it's no surprised that I never married.

I did the same at work. For example, I got a promotion but was afraid that if I showed joy, they'd think I felt I didn't deserve the promotion. Or they'd think they could underpay me. Or— and it was probably irrational— my jealous former supervisees would more likely try to sabotage me.

I even showed nothing when I got my cancer diagnosis— a death sentence. The doctor even said, "You seem to be taking it in stride." Inside, I was terrified but said only, "Well, we all have to go sometime."

I told no one about the cancer. Not only did I not want to burden anyone with it, if they did something nice for me, I'd feel I had to reciprocate and didn't have the energy. Again, that's probably irrational but I want to tell you my truth.

The only way my sister found out is that when I collapsed, vomiting blood, I had to call 911 and, in the hospital, they looked in my wallet and saw that my sister was listed as next-of-kin.

She asked, "Why didn't you tell me?"

For a rare time, I smiled and said, "You think about it."

An Empty Nester

I had been an unofficial empty-nester during Amber's last two years of high school. She cared mainly about her friends, her boyfriend, and her phone. Me? The source of three hots, a cot, cash, and car.

Easterstock Photos, Freelmageslive, CC3.0

But this was the moment I became official. I pulled into the dorm parking lot to drop off Amber for her first year at college. I went to help her with her bags but she shooed me away. I wanted to feel useful and distract myself from the coming moment but she'd have none of it.

"Bye, mother."

"Good luck, Amber."

"It's Ember. I want to be called Ember." "Right, Ember. Call, would you?"

Sure, mother."

And without a second look, she grabbed her duffel bag in one hand, dragged her trunk with the other, and that was that.

It was an hour's drive back to the airport and then a six-hour flight back to San Francisco, so I had plenty of time to think, maybe too much time.

I was reminded that Amber's first big insult— the obligatory, "I hate you, mother!" doesn't count— was when she insisted she is going back east for college.

That's shorthand for, "As far away from me as possible." Damn it, I was a good mother. No one's perfect but I was better to her and gave her a better life than 90% of two-parent families. She won't call me much, except for money. I'll be lucky to see her at Christmas.

Now all I have is Woogie my dog) a couple friends, and my job. It's a good job—marketing manager for a quality skincare company, but that isn't enough.

What if I moved near Amber? I mean, Ember. Not so close that she'd feel hovered but if she wanted to, she could come over for dinner one night or even for the weekend.

I could get a nice little cottage with enough room to plant vegetables and for Woogie to run around. Maybe I'd find new friends, maybe even a guy. Men-women relationships in San Francisco are so fraught. And because housing is much cheaper in Western Massachusetts, I could quit my job and work in a bookstore or a cafe. Or maybe I'd open a bookstore cafe.

I lived with all that through the drive, even through TSA, and onto the plane. But when the flight attendant said, "We've passed through 10,000 feet. You're free to use your electronic devices," I opened my laptop and started to look at a spreadsheet, but couldn't make myself.

Like Mother, Like Daughter?

I wanted to be sure that my daughter, Crystal, would live up to her potential. She gets mainly Bs on her report cards, so I emailed her teacher asking for her to get tested for the gifted program.

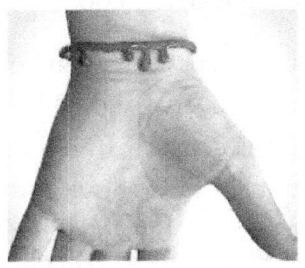
Oddity, CC0

But the teacher emailed me that she thinks Crystal is an overachiever, working hard, creating neat and thorough work, but that her reasoning ability— key to giftedness— is pretty average.

I didn't want to accept that. Looking back, that was because I was scared that was true of me and that I only got an Ivy League degree because I killed myself. So I demanded that Crystal be tested for the gifted program.

When the school psychologist emailed me— I guess she couldn't face me— Crystal scored just slightly above average.

Still, I wanted to be sure I was giving Crystal every opportunity. So I asked if she could try being in the after-school program for gifted kids. They said no ... until I threatened to sue. I guess that scared them, so they agreed.

But that turned out to be my bad. Crystal struggled there and at the end of class on just the second day, when the kids were let out to the schoolyard to go home, one kid pointed to Crystal and said, "Too dumb." Other kids thought that was funny and so they chimed in and circled her: "Too dumb! Too dumb!! Too dumb!!!"

I figured, okay, maybe that wasn't' the right program for Crystal, so I signed her up for the after-school Math for Girls course offered by a local girl-empowerment nonprofit. I thought that maybe I was pushing Crystal too hard, but when I saw her working hard on her Math for Girls homework in addition to her regular homework, I felt okay.

But not for long. One night, just before bedtime, I heard her crying in her bedroom. The door was locked, I knocked, and she yelled, "Go away!" I kept knocking and finally she screamed, "See if I care!" She opened the door and I saw that her wrist was slit. But it turns out it was fake— It was a decal she had bought on the Internet.

I sent her to counseling, and then I went too. I've since eased up and I think that will make her more successful and definitely happier. To tell the truth, I'm also easing up on myself.

A Pregnant Nod

Jen finished her last fight of the day. She told the author, "You really should use 'unimportant,' not 'nugatory.'" Such wasn't in Jen's fantasy when she dreamt of being in book publishing. But proofreader is as far as she has gotten.

With permission, 18/1 Graphics Studio

And now at 38, because of some combination of personal choice, peer pressure, and the tick-tock of her bio clock, Jen's priority was on becoming a mom.

Jen would love a partner but her track record says, "Long shot." So she visited a sperm bank. She thought, "I'm going just to look." Those are dangerous words, like when someone says they're going to the animal shelter just to look.

After reviewing dozens of profiles and mulling how much to compromise on the sperm donor's intelligence, looks, and personality, she settled on #462.

Kyle was born normal, but a normal baby is an abnormal challenge, for example, hours of inexplicable crying and the resulting sleep-deprived mom who, in this case, stopped giving a shit about whether the comma should go inside or outside the parenthesis.

After just three days, Jen told her mom that she's thinking of giving the baby up for adoption. Whether or not that was a ploy, it worked and Grandma offered to sacrifice her new empty-nester freedom for parenthood round two.

But in just days, when Jen came home and reached out her arms hoping that Kyle would be eager to see her, he nuzzled into Grandma— every night. So Jen cut back working to half-time.

One day, Jen sat bored on a park bench with Kyle in the stroller, her brain going to mush. A guy pushing a stroller asked if the empty spot on the bench was available. She thought, "Is he unshaven because he's cool or slovenly?" and muttered, "Okay, I guess."

Talky, he said he was divorced and wished he could meet a working woman so he could quit his job and be a house husband.

Internally, Jen screamed. I don't want this guy. I don't want to be a parent. I don't want to go back to work. I don't know what the hell I want."

But all she did was nod.

A Terrible Two

One sperm got to the egg ahead of the other billions. And that's how Jason was born. As usual, the cells divided and grew, which may be the universe's greatest mystery.

With permission, 18/1 Graphics Studio

In Jason's 25th week, he became sentient and thought, "What's all this?" There was mom's heartbeat and stomach gurglings, and, of course, the warm, moist womb. He thought, "I'm curious."

After nine months, "What's this?" And he was moved toward the light. "Oh, goody!"

Dad was there but only out of responsibility— He was divorcing her. His explanation: "I feel trapped." Mom, ever efficient, now would have to be more so. She even raced out of the hospital.

As soon as Jason was old enough to listen, mom imposed maximum efficiency on him. "No" was the operative and most frequent word.

By age 2, Jason had had enough. He was going to take control. At first, it was standard stuff, for example, "I don't want broccoli. I want ice cream!" and when mom insisted, "No!" he dumped the broccoli onto the floor.

But Jason had bigger plans: He had long enjoyed looking out the window to see the cars, the people, "a whole world I want to see!" And at two, he decided he would. He knew his mother would never let him go out by himself and, with her, it was mainly: get strapped into the car seat, into the supermarket, strapped in again, and back home. "Boring!"

So when Jason's mother was working in her home-office, he sneaked to the front door and turned the lock. Mom's hearing was fine and after a moment of resentment of having to stop working, she shot to the door and yelled, you guessed it, "No!"

She locked the deadbolt and thought, "That's too high. Jason can't reach it," and rushed back to her work.

The "No!" only strengthened Jason's resolve. He waited a few minutes until she was fully immersed in work. Then, he pulled out the toy broom she had given him for his birthday— "No gender-stereotyped roles for my son!" He tiptoed to the door, more quietly unlocked the doorknob, and then used the broom to unlatch the deadbolt.

Screech! Mom looked out the window to see a car that was just a foot from Jason. She raced out, yelled the usual, "No!" but with maximum fervor, dragged him into his room, and locked the door.

Jason surveyed his room, saw the skylight, opened the dresser drawers, stepped on the bottom one and started climbing.

Bully

Michael's mother regretted not aborting him. There were the small things, like his too-quickly outgrowing his clothes, which was no surprise given that his father was a football player. But more aggravating was that Michael was a bully. He wasn't mean. He just needed lots of stimulation, adrenaline rushes. So he chased and threatened kids, towering over them with his hulkish body but never hit them. Well, once he did, but the kid truly deserved it.

With permission, 18/1 Graphics Studio

Michael got expelled from the 5th grade for pulling a girl's bra strap. The principal insisted, "That is a violation of the district's policy of zero tolerance of sexual harassment."

Michael hated home schooling, and being around his mother all the time made her resent him even more. It became a vicious cycle: She'd yell at him, even hit him with a belt, which made him want to make her angry, which would increase her venom.

Despite the beatings, Michael would, for example, play handball against the living room wall even when she'd yell, "Stop it. You'll break something!" He wouldn't stop and she whipped him.

Michael wasn't brave enough to run away. As I said, he acted tough but really, despite his mother's strictures, he valued the structure of home, meals he could count on, and perhaps most of all, sleeping in his bed with his teddy bear tucked under his arm just right.

At 7 the next morning, Michael's mother stomped into his room, brandishing the belt. She threw off his blanket, fired his teddy bear against the wall, and yelled. "I wake up and what do I see? My prize vase, broken! I TOLD you not to play ball in the house!" She whipped him and stormed out.

Scared of running away but more eager to punish his mother, Michael gathered his sleeping bag, the $37 in allowance he had saved, and stuffed his canteen, a fleece, and toothpaste into his backpack. He checked to be sure his mother wasn't in the kitchen, then raced in and stuffed a bag of trail mix into his pack, at which point, his mother came in from the bathroom. "And just where do you think you're going?"

Michael didn't answer, strode through the back door, hopped on his bike, and left for Berkeley, the place his teacher called, "the most progressive place on earth." Michael didn't know what "progressive" meant but it sounded good and Berkeley was only 30 miles from home yet far enough that his mother and the cops would have a hard time finding him.

On the way, Michael almost got run over twice, once in San Leandro when a driver opened his parked car door without looking, the other time in Oakland when a driver changed lanes within inches of Michael. He fell off his bike and, heart thumping, got back on and pedaled hard.

Seeing the brown "Entering Berkeley' sign was the first time Michael thought about where to put his sleeping bag: In a doorway? Under a freeway overpass? He didn't have to think long because he soon came upon a large homeless encampment filled with tents and strewn garbage.

The residents ignored Michael, and he put his bike and sleeping bag under a tree. Exhausted, even though it was only 8 PM, he went to sleep. Ten hours later, the sunrise woke him. His bike was gone and, after a half hour wandering the camp to try to find it, he gave up.

Michael saw three men trudge from the encampment toward the library across the street and he thought, "Hmm, homeless people like to read? So do I, especially Harry Potter." So he followed them. But when they entered, they didn't head to the shelves or even to the magazine section. They went into the bathroom and Michael followed. There, they used the toilet, washed their underarms in the sink, and one guy filled a 40-ounce SuperBigGulp 7-11 cup with water.

The men left the library but Michael stayed to explore. He stopped at the computers, googled "dinosaurs" and watched National Geographic's Dinosaurs 101 and then the BBC's Top Five Ferocious Dinosaur Moments. He thought, "I learned more about dinosaurs in that half hour than in the whole month we spent on dinosaurs in school, it was much more fun, and I didn't need to sit in my seat for hours at a time."

Michael went outside, people-watched and window-shopped, then sat on a bench, ate some trail mix, and washed it down with water from his canteen.

He bought a blank notecard and wrote, "I'll come home, probably."

So his mother and the cops would have a harder time finding him, he asked a passerby where the nearest post office in Oakland is. He walked the two miles, bought a Mickey Mouse stamp from the vending machine, and mailed it. He thought, "That should teach her a lesson."

Mush

My wife's career is skyrocketing and mine sputtered, so I didn't mind offering to be househusband and when Mia arrived, Mr. Mom.

Helena Lopes, Pexels, CC0

I've been doing it for seven years now and can say that, yes, being a homemaker with a kid is a full-time job, but at least the work isn't difficult. And when Mia is in school, I do have time to go out to lunch with friends, hit the gym, and volunteer in Mia's school. It's a nice life.

Recently, Emily— that's my wife— came home from work excited: "I found a good job for you. It's at my company. They have Python programmers but they need a legacy programmer— Java. You know that!"

I said, "I appreciate it, Emily, but to be honest, because I've been a homemaker so long, not only are my Java skills rusty, no, rusted, I feel my brain has gone to mush. I'm happy as a househusband and Mr. Mom. Emily, I should look in on Sammy. She probably needs changing."

Buried Treasure

It was standard dad-teen stuff: He wanted nothing to do with me. And soon, he'd be off to college, so I figured I'd offer a father-son bonding trip he couldn't refuse.

Conklinj, Wikimedia, CC 4.0

I suggested we rent a submersible, hire a pilot, and go search for the crates of gold coins that are buried 240 feet deep in the ocean 50 miles off the Nantucket coast.

How did all those gold coins end up there? In 1909, the SS Florida collided into a British cruise ship, the RMS Republic. Attempts to find the coins have failed, but the new, better, and less expensive-to-rent submersibles improve the chances. Even so, I seriously doubted we'd succeed where many had failed, not to mention the recent fatal attempt on The Titanic.

And we didn't succeed. All we found were wine bottles, a toilet, and a human skull, a helluva souvenir though. When we got back home, we were in the living room, staring at the skull.

My son said, "Dad, that's what I'll look like after I die." I nodded and said, "It's a memento mori."

He said, "What's that?"

"A reminder that we should do all we can while we can."

He asked, "Have fun? Work a lot? Balance? He with the most toys wins?"

"Everyone has their own formula. What's yours?"

"I don't know."

I said, "Think."

"Yeah, I need to think about it."

Friends

The Broken Hearts Club

It wasn't much of a club actually—only three members. But we like it despite or probably because we're all women.

Andrew Demenyuk, Attributed Free License, Deposit Photos

Jeannie has pined for guy after guy but none of them wanted her as more than, as she put it, "a sperm receptacle." She continued, "I'm jealous of all those women with rings on their fingers, prancing around with their baby carriages." Tina asked, "Are you sure you're not better off without all that—Remember, better solo than so-so."

Relationship Stories

Heather's husband died in, as she put it, "a fucking motorcycle accident." She said that now six months later, "I'm still grieving. I can't make myself do anything." Jeannie asked, "Is that just an excuse? If so, for what?"

Tina's off-again/on-again boyfriend is, as she put it, "off permanently." She exclaimed, "I was so perfect?" Heather asked, "Would he agree?"

Mainly, the Broken Hearts Club grouses, occasionally about their insecurities but mainly as Jeannie said and the others agreed, that "men suck." Society's mind-molders—the colleges and especially the media — promulgate that. So "men suck" has become an ever more hard-wired "truth."

But all three members knew that, as Heather said, "Bitching does no good. Let's move forward." So while they found it more fun to complain, they were, as Tina said, "Good, bad-ass women" and they discussed how to move forward.

Jeannie promised not to go to bed with a guy until at least the third date.

Heather swore, "No more bad boys."

Tina said, "I need to make myself stop thinking about Tony and start putting myself out there again."

They all agreed that guys just aren't that important, even if one doesn't suck.

The Broken Hearts Club meets in a cafe and, today, a guy, a cute guy, ambled over. He smiled, "I'm bad—I've been listening to you. Could I sit in?"

Jeannie pursed her lips. Heather flushed. Tina giggled.

My Hero

Before I started to get interested in girls, I loved to watch baseball. My hero was a Yankee named Bill Thurmond. He was such a powerful hitter and his arm!— He could throw out a runner at the plate from deep left field!

Keith JJ, Pixabay, Free to use

I was watching the post-game press conference after the Yankees had beaten the Dodgers. I was happy and even happier when Bill, who had hit the walk-off home run, was on. The press conference was almost over when a reporter asked, "So Bill, what are you doing for the community?"

Bill hesitated and looked over to the Yankees' PR person who sat beside him, and she said, "Bill will be giving kids a lesson on success and a tour of the clubhouse this Saturday morning at 10."

I couldn't wait. I was there at 9:30. Already a dozen kids were lined up at the locker room's front door. At 10:00 they let us in and the PR person was there but not Thurmond—I figured he had a busy schedule so he was

Relationship Stories

running late. At 10:15, with a beautiful woman on his arm, Bill walked in. Actually, he trudged in. Was he hurt?

The PR person introduced him to us kids. Why did his face look so sleepy? Or was it sad? Did he have a hangover? Was he on drugs? Anyway, I couldn't wait to hear what he would teach us. It ended up being very short. He slurred, "You kids, work hard in school and at baseball and you can be a star. Everyone is a star. You just gotta believe it."

And with that, he started to trudge out, his lady friend tagging behind. A kid called out, "Hey, you're supposed to give us a tour." Bill slurred, "Vanessa will."

I was disappointed.

Vanessa, the PR person, gave us the tour and that made me teary. The equipment manager saw my sad face, got down to my height, and asked me what was wrong. I explained that Bill's lesson was so short and he didn't say anything I thought would be helpful. Then, not only did he break his promise to give us the tour, the tour made me see that a major-league locker room is just another smelly room with metal lockers kind of like in my school's gym."

The equipment manager said, "Wait a minute" and he came back with a brand-new pair of sanitary socks, the socks the players wear between their stirrups and cleats, and it was signed "Bill Thurmond." The equipment manager said to me, "Bill said to give this to a special kid. You're it."

I left happy until, at home, I compared the signature with the one on Bill Thurmond's baseball card. They were different. To cover for Bill and because he felt sorry for me, the equipment manager must have signed it. I have never thought about heroes the same way.

Following Church Teachings

I was putting out my jello mold for the church supper. To avoid it being the stereotype and to make it a little healthier, I made it in a heart-shaped mold and mixed in fresh cherries, well, frozen cherries, defrosted. But that's beside the point.

With permission, 18/1 Graphics Studio

Next to me, putting out her tuna casserole was a woman I didn't know well, around my age, 35. I couldn't even remember her name, so I was glad when she was kind enough to not assume I knew it. She said, "Hi Mary, I'm Christine."

I prefer to be quiet but she was a talker, and before I knew it, she was telling me that she needed to move out of her apartment and was having trouble finding one she could afford, even a share.

Maybe it was because two weeks ago, the minister did the sermon on generosity. She quoted something from Corinthians, something like, "Each of you should give, and not reluctantly, for God loves a cheerful giver."

So without really thinking, I put on my churchy smile and said, "How'd you like to share my apartment? I'll only charge you $500 a month." No surprise, she jumped at it.

As soon as she did, doubts crept in: What if she plays loud music? What if she leaves the kitchen messy? And sharing a bathroom— I'll have to smell her, well, you know.

But I didn't anticipate this: Every night, there were, well, intimacy noises. Loud ones. They were especially loud when she had company but even when she was alone.

It wasn't just the noise, it was the reminder that, for some reason, I've never enjoyed sex that much. I certainly don't crave it. It's not because of guilt, even though when I was growing up, I still remember the Sunday School teacher pointing to the cross and only half— kidding saying, "This is what happens if you have premarital sex." When you're in the sixth grade, you kind of take such warnings literally. At least I did.

I tried to be Christian about it. I endured Christine's enthusiasms as long as I could without saying anything. After all, it would be unchristian of me to deny her pleasure, especially in her own home, even if it was my home too.

Then I tried raising the issue in a loving way: "I'm pleased that you feel comfortable living as you'd like, but I'm wondering if you just might be just a bit quieter when you're, well, enjoying yourself. Or at least put some music on so I'm not hearing quite as much." She was Christian about it and said she felt terrible that I've caused pain and promised to be quieter. And she was for a while but then started up again.

I hoped it would be just temporary, but no. So I tried again, this time, just a bit less kindly: "Christine, I'm having difficulty with the noise. It's even making it hard to sleep. So I'm hoping..."

A few weeks more of ever less kind begging and then I did what I'd think Jesus would think is the most Christian thing. I said, "Christine, I am pleased that you are happy here. I don't need this apartment that badly. It's yours. I'll find another place."

The Garden Club

We meet in a member's garden, Julia's, around the fire pit. We loved our meetings…if it wasn't for Eleanor. Not two minutes went by before Eleanor would brag about her garden or ridicule ours. And one night, Julia caught Eleanor spraying Julia's prize roses with herbicide! But it was too late: Julia lost the gorgeous and rare roses, Sheer Elegance, Black Magic, and Yves Piaget. Dead, gone!

Travel4FoodFun, Pixabay, Public Domain

We politely asked Eleanor to quit: "We're not sure we're the best fit." But at the next meeting, there was Eleanor, more obnoxious than ever. She told one member, "You're a senile old bitty who can't even grow a marigold!" That was the last straw. By acclimation, we agreed to expel her from the club. But Eleanor seethed, "Do that and I'll sue your asses. I will be at your meetings until the day I die." She didn't know how right she was.

We debated what to do: Let her stay and ruin our club? Try to get a restraining order? The judge would laugh us out of court—"You're taking up the court's time because you don't like a member of your garden club?!"

We decided we needed to get rid of Eleanor. It would serve the common good—not just our club's but if she was so damaging to a garden club, she was probably even moreso to more important things and people.

We know plants, so we put poppy extract in her tea— Yes, the same kind as in the Wizard of Oz. It's an opioid. That put her into a deep sleep. Then we burned her in the fire pit.

The police interviewed us but it was perfunctory. After all, we're just a bunch of "senile old bitties." When the cops left, we celebrated by sprinkling Eleanor's ashes around the plants. It's good fertilizer, high in potash.

The Hillcrest Widow Club

The four women of the Hillcrest Widow Club met every Thursday morning at 9 in the corner of a quiet coffee shop.

Gareth Williams, Flickr, CC2.0

Their statements about their deceased husbands started politely. For example, Mary said, "Yes, it's difficult but I'm trying to muddle through."

But slowly, their fear of being seen as cold faded, but what really opened things up was when Zoe said, "Honestly, I'm relieved to be rid of that ball and chain."

Britney then felt free to pile on: "Don't we like talking with each other rather than with men? "We care more about family, feelings, and okay, fashion. The successful men mainly want to talk about their work, the unsuccessful ones about stupid sports."

Further emboldened, Zoe said, "And they just care about getting in and out, assuming they can get it up, which for the last decade, my husband at least couldn't. And I had to pretend it was okay." Two of the other women nodded.

That encouraged Zoe to admit that she had fantasies about lesbian sex, okay, more than fantasies.

Before long, they decided they needed more privacy, so they met in Zoe's plush living room. Mary asked, "How could you afford this?" Zoe replied, "My husband was a lawyer who had one client but a great one: the Environmental Protection Agency."

After a glass of wine or a bong hit, Zoe moved close to Willow, the member who seemed most likely to be willing to kiss. Zoe looked her in the eye and when Willow didn't avert, Zoe kissed her as the others watched wide-eyed. Would Willow pull back? On the contrary, she sighed in pleasure.

But Zoe sensed it was too fast, not just for Willow, but for the others. So Zoe pulled back and asked if someone would like another hit or glass of wine.

But three "Zoe meetings" later, they all, and I mean all, had a very cuddly experience. But after, Mary whispered something that shocked the others:

I love our Widow's Club but every so often I wonder, "Are men so bad that we're fine with bashing them. We wouldn't criticize women, let alone BIPOCs. If I did, I'd get the 3C's: Censure, Censor, or Cancel. Atop that, in so many news shows and especially movies, TV shows, and novels, a spunky, smart woman usually triumphs over an evil or clueless guy. And when women have the deficit, say, we're so-called underrepresented in science, there's massive redress and, yes, reverse discrimination— I know a number of women who got jobs over more competent, harder-working guys. Okay, so did I. Yet when men have the ultimate deficit— They live six(!) years shorter than women, their last decade in worse health, and there are 4.4 widows for every widower— all we see is another run for breast cancer."

Over the next few meetings, the others began to shun Mary. It was subtle: a little less eye contact, a little more interrupting, and unlike before, no one asked her to get together between meetings.

Sad at being ostracized, Mary figured, "It's not that big a deal to play the game." She even told anti-male jokes: "What do you call a man with half a brain? Gifted. What's the difference between government bonds and men? Bonds mature. What is the difference between a man and a catfish? One is a bottom-feeding scum-sucker and the other is a fish."

Soon, Mary was back in the fold.

Dogs

Kisser

The doorbell rang at 3 AM. I opened the door to find a wicker basket. In it, wrapped in a blanket, was a puppy.

Liz West, Flickr, CC 2.0

I work full-time. Who has time for a dog? Even if I got a dogsitter—that's expensive and then there are the nights and the weekends.

And the training! Who has time? Who wants pee and poop in the house?

So cute as the puppy was, I steeled myself, carried him into the car and drove to the pound.

Relationship Stories

He would not get off my lap. Indeed, the more I drove, the more he curled up in my lap. And then he fell asleep on my lap.

Still, I was not going to have a dog!

I pulled into the pound's parking lot, saw the entrance—It reminded me of Auschwitz. I pursed my lips and lifted the puppy with one hand and started to reach for the car door with the other. And then, damn it, the puppy licked my face.

I just couldn't do it. I closed the car door, yeah with the puppy and me inside. I named it based on what just happened. My forever companion would be named Kisser.

But if it was one thing I wouldn't let Kisser do is disrupt my sleep. So even before I got home, I went to the pet store and got a crate and a cushion to put inside it. Add the food, collar and leash, and tax and I was out $247. And that was before the vet visit. Perfectly healthy but needing spaying and shots—another 300 bucks.

I read on the internet how important it is to begin housebreaking immediately and to count on it taking a week. So damn it, I took a week off from work. And every time Kisser got up from his nap, I carried him outside to the pee place and waited… and waited. Finally, success, followed instantly by a treat and massive praise. But despite my diligence, Kisser had a few accidents, including one vomit. But yes, after a week he was trained.

But Kisser would not sleep in his crate. The first night, I put him in and within seconds, he was whimpering, the sweetest damn whimper you ever heard. I needed to sleep so I moved the crate from the kitchen to my bedroom. He still whimpered, and whimpered. At some God-forsaken hour, I got up, put a towel on the far corner of the bed—I was NOT going to have pee or poop on my blanket—and I lowered him onto the towel. He immediately stopped whimpering, curled up and went to sleep—He was doing a great job of training me. The only thing, by the time I got up in the morning, Kisser was no longer at the foot of the bed. He was curled up around my warmest spot—my crotch. And when I started to get up, he jumped on me, licked my face, we went out, and he did his business like a pro.

After a week, I was grateful I had Kisser. I could see why they call a dog man's best friend. So you can imagine how I felt when after eight days, the doorbell rang. It was a neighbor. She said, "I had just gotten a puppy when, in the middle of the night, I got a call from a hospital 200 miles away—My dad had had a heart attack. I was frantic. I was so frantic I forget to leave you a note and I forgot all about the dog. My dad died, we had the funeral, and when I came back and saw the crate, I remembered. I am so sorry, so so sorry. Thank you so much for taking care of my puppy. Can I have him back now?"

Second Love

I was retiring— People don't want a 75-year-old dentist. Sometimes, I wonder who my patients will miss more— me or Naomi my tiny, furry dirigible that sat on patients' laps while I was drilling, pulling, root-canaling.

This is my dog, Hachi. Photo credit: own work.

Naomi too was at retirement age. She was 17. As I sat home on my first day of retirement, Naomi on my lap, I felt bad for her. She always had the stimulation of a parade of patients every day. Now she was stuck with just me. Should I get another dog? Am I too old? And with Naomi 17, maybe it would be good to have a young dog to ease my pain when Naomi goes. That held sway and I signed up for alerts from 24PetConnect.com, PetFinder.com, and AdoptaPet.com, which aggregate listings of available dogs from dozens of shelters.

Mainly there were pit bulls and chihuahuas, not my type. But finally, a sweet little puffball named Angel came available. When I took Angel for the test walk, I introduced her to Naomi and it was love at first sight. And in the car, Naomi somehow knew that Angel wanted to be on my lap, so Naomi just curled up on the passenger seat. I lifted Angel onto my lap and she rested her head on my thigh as though we'd done that for years.

The three of us did great. Angel would run around Naomi to get her to play and for a while she did. But then, Naomi slowed down further, and even when Angel would paw at her to play, Naomi would barely raise her head, and then not even that. And then Naomi lost continence.

I took Naomi to the vet. Of course, Angel came with us. Angel, like Naomi, came everywhere with me. Before leaving the car, I hugged Angel, for my benefit more than hers, and went in. The vet had that sad look when I asked, "Naomi is 18. Is it time?" She nodded and asked if I wanted to stay in the room. I did— I didn't want her last moments to be without me. The vet gently gave the injection and the already sleepy Naomi went to her final sleep. Then the vet asked if I'd like to stay in the room a while. She left, I cried, and then found myself pounding the wall in agony. Finally, when I got just a bit of control, I padded out into the waiting room, still teary.

A woman who had just left the other exam room with her puppy intuited what happened, and hugged me. I don't know if it was my vulnerability but I stayed for a few moments in her arms, my head on her shoulders. Then she lifted my head, we looked into each other's eyes, and then she did the last thing I thought she would. She asked, "Would you like to go out for coffee?" And that's how she, her dog Sweetheart, my dog Angel, and I started dating.

Made in the USA
Las Vegas, NV
21 August 2023

76371876R00085